TWENTY-ONE
CARDINALS

TWENTY-ONE
CARDINALS

JOCELYNE SAUCIER

translated by Rhonda Mullins

Coach House Books, Toronto

Saucier

First English edition. Originally published in French in 1999 as *Les héritiers de la mine* by Les Éditions XYZ inc.

first edition

 Canada Council   Conseil des Arts
for the Arts   du Canada

 ONTARIO ARTS COUNCIL
CONSEIL DES ARTS DE L'ONTARIO
an Ontario government agency
un organisme du gouvernement de l'Ontario

 Canadä

Coach House Books acknowledges the financial support of the Government of Canada through the National Translation Program for Book Publishing for our translation activities. Published with the generous assistance of the Canada Council for the Arts and the Ontario Arts Council. We also acknowledge the support of the Government of Canada through the Canada Book Fund.

LIBRARY AND ARCHIVES CANADA CATALOGUING IN PUBLICATION

Saucier, Jocelyne, 1948-
[Héritiers de la mine. English]
    Twenty-one Cardinals / Jocelyne Saucier ; translated by Rhonda Mullins.

Translation of: Les héritiers de la mine.
ISBN 978-1-55245-307-0 (pbk.)

    I. Mullins, Rhonda, 1966-, translator II. Title. III. Title: Héritiers de la mine. English.

PS8587.A38633H4713 2015   C843'.54   C2014-908409-9

Twenty-One Cardinals is available as an ebook: ISBN 978 1 77056 407 7

Purchase of the print version of this book entitles you to a free digital copy. To claim your ebook of this title, please email sales@chbooks.com with proof of purchase or visit chbooks.com/digital. (Coach House Books reserves the right to terminate the free digital download offer at any time.)

for Gilles

When the old coot with the nicotine-stained teeth asked the question, I knew we were headed back to the good ol' days.

I have no problem with that. I love it when I feel our family slip into the conversation and I know someone is going to ask the question.

My family has always fascinated me and given me a leg up in conversations. We're nothing like other families. We are self-made. We are an essence unto ourselves, unique and dissonant, the only members of our species. Livers of humdrum lives who flitted around us got their wings burned. We're not mean, but we can bare our teeth. People didn't hang around when a band of Cardinals made its presence known.

'There were how many of you?'

The question invokes tales of wonder, and I have wonder to spare. I don't know if I manage to conceal my pride when I hear them repeat in a chorus, stunned, in awe:

'Twenty-one? Twenty-one kids?'

The other questions come on the heels of the first, always the same ones, or pretty much. How did we manage meals? How big was the table? (It's always a woman who wants to know.) Where did we live? How many bedrooms were there? What was Christmas like? The start of a new school year? A new baby? And your mother, wasn't she worn out from carrying all those children?

So I tell them. About the house our father had moved from Perron to Norcoville after he discovered the mine. The four kitchens, the four living rooms, the four tiny bathrooms – which we called the wc, for *water closet*, because there was no bath or sink. It was a house made up of four apartments; our father had merely broken down the walls. I lay it on thick. The two dozen eggs in the morning, the hundred pounds of potatoes in the cellar, the morning battles to find our boots, the evening battles for a place in front of the TV, the constant battles for nothing, for fun, out of habit. The good ol' days.

I tell them everything I've been told. I missed the best part of our family's life, when we were Big, when we were pretty much all still at home and had stars in our eyes about what awaited us once we left Norco one by one and set off to conquer the world. The era of Geronimo, Big Yellow, Tommy, El Toro. The 1960s. The mine was closed, Norco was crumbling, the houses were disappearing – they were either moved or we had burnt them down – scrub was taking over the cement foundations, weeds ate away at the pot-holed roads. We reigned over Norco, which should have been called Cardinal, because it was our father who discovered the zinc that was extracted from the mine, and they stole it from him.

I wasn't yet born when the mine closed. There was dismay, dejection and wailing from the shacks, but not at our house. This was our moment. Northern Consolidated had just been tripped up by international finance and was being dragged along behind the plummeting price of zinc. It had reached the bottom and wet itself. We weren't going to shed any tears. Our mine had been returned to us.

I was born one year later, a pointy-headed runt, which necessarily made me the last, the twenty-first, nicknamed the Caboose. When my father saw the howling bag of bones in the cradle (because of the forceps? because I was marring his lineage?), he decided there would be no more.

The last one, the Caboose, always being carted around on hips, on shoulders, passed hand to hand, constantly howling, screaming and crying, afraid of being left behind somewhere. Good lord, how I wailed and cried! I think about it and I can still feel my larynx tighten, wanting to open up, the burning air of a cry that swelled, expanded, built to pierce the highest note and persisted even once someone had grabbed me by the collar or the sleeve and dragged me along to wherever they were all going, a great throng of Cardinals big and small, ready to tackle another outrageous plan.

I wasn't really crying. I was protesting. Protesting being so small, so frail and so defenceless. Being so unlike a Cardinal. The others ran errands in minus-thirty-degree weather, barefoot in the snow, while I had a toque jammed down over my ears as soon as the slightest cool weather hit in the fall, because of recurrent ear infections. They would compare their frostbite the next day, and I was asked to palpate the swollen soles of their feet to see who had the best blisters from the cold. They would limp for a few days, but if one of them grimaced in pain, the others would burst out laughing.

They were thin, but with muscles and nerves stretched taut, as if they were ready to pounce, always on alert, at the starting line of a race or watching for prey they would make short work of.

We were a race of conquerors. Of those who do not bend or break, of those who follow their instinct, who spread their wings wide and fly in the face of fear. We were the kings of Norco.

I was under their wing, and I had nothing to fear but being forgotten in the fray. There were so many of us.

Sometimes we would head out in a group of eight or ten. We would be off to set fire to an abandoned house, hunt small critters or whatever else. They would never tell me. And then, all of a sudden, without me knowing why, the group would split up. Three or four would follow El Toro or Tintin or Big Yellow, while the others ran through the dry grass, and I would be left alone in a huge field dotted with the remains of homes. I would feel space distend and a cry of panic scratch at my throat. Often, I wouldn't even have yelled yet, and I would hear: 'Grab the Caboose!' It was usually Tintin. He would realize that I had become separated from the expedition and send Wapiti or one of the Weewuns to my rescue.

I was five, maybe six, and the town seemed to go on forever. Yet I simply had to stand on the sheet metal roof of the dynamite shed, which we would slide down winter and summer, and I could see the entire expanse of it. From the disused fire station that gleamed white in the sun (it was built just before the mine closed) to the flimsy hovels scattered along the forest's edge, there were three large, square, grassy plots of land and, lost in the desolation, a few houses in ruins or well on their way. It was the same when you looked along the other axis: space, tall grass, grey asphalt roads full of potholes, a few forsaken buildings and, just about anywhere you looked, the mounds left by houses that had been transported elsewhere: the cement foundations, the sagging sheds, the body of a car that didn't want to follow. And sometimes, lo and behold, a smart, tidy house cultivating flowers and hubris. Like the Potvins', which had once been the city hall. Just two children. The son was going to college, the daughter to the convent, and their mother played the organ at church. Rich people we cheerfully despised.

Norco had shrunk since the closing of the mine. There had once been a movie theatre, two garages, restaurants, grocery stores. All that was left was the fire station, the rink with its shelter for the benches, the church and its presbytery, a restaurant/corner store/post office, and, the thing that always surprises people when I tell them, two hotels and three schools.

The schools tell the tale of what people had hoped for from Norco. A mining town that would attract prosperity, longevity and happiness for its children. The dream didn't last, and we had to make do with disillusionment and three large, handsome red brick schools. And so every morning, a dozen school buses brought children from neighbouring villages. They were the children of hicks, who had to milk cows and muck out stables, untrained in the art of idleness, no taste for freedom. They let themselves be saddled and ridden, and they were ours for the day.

I hesitate here when I tell the story, because often I'm speaking to people who had childhoods similar to those of the hicks.

We weren't the local bullies. We didn't go about insulting people, tripping them, bloodying noses. Of course, we wouldn't walk away from a good fight – hand-to-hand battle, like a duel. Eye to eye, muscles raging, well-landed blows imparted and received, the pain that makes you even angrier. It was intoxicating.

Nor were we the sort to pull down little girls' panties or steal marbles. We were the kings. The real deal. We wanted so much from ourselves and from life that everything around us seemed pathetic.

So the hicks, with their dull minds, their diligent understanding of nothing at all and their general insignificance, were a constant source of wonder. We couldn't stop marvelling at their stupidity and our intelligence.

Geronimo was the smartest. Pure, distilled Cardinal. The story goes that he was the one who started the anti-hick commandos, the bear blasting and the festival of cats. When I manage to get someone talking (we aren't talkative, except for me, who is always trying to bring the conversation 'round to our life in Norco), I can be sure Geronimo will show up at the climax of the story and, no matter who is doing the telling, I always know it will end the same way, in the same admiring tone: 'He was the smartest Cardinal.'

He was just thirteen or fourteen when he started accompanying our father to his claims. He would leave at the crack of dawn, his prospecting gear in a yellow canvas bag slung over his shoulder, gesturing with his hand to everyone at the breakfast table – a gesture meant mainly for the older ones to mark the distance that separated them now that he was roaming the woods with our father. He would come back late at night, dirty, beat, famished, and if he had to go back to school the next day, he would retreat into a sullen funk. He dropped out in Grade 9.

No one took offence when our father made him his assistant. He was the smartest, but also, as Mustang once told me, he was the one most interested in rocks. 'He had been studying rocks long before he was chosen. As soon as he saw the Old Man head down to the basement, he would follow him and stay there for hours watching him inspect and scratch his samples. You could hear them talking, Geronimo asking questions and the Old Man explaining.'

I often went down to the basement to daydream about our father discovering an incredible mine from one of his rocks. He had hundreds and hundreds of them, labelled and categorized by origin in baskets piled on planks hanging askew along the west wall. What I saw fuelled my admiration for our father. I knew nothing of rhyolite, galenite, copper pyrites, all the precious words written in his own hand, but I liked to read them and imagine that he was sharing his secrets with me.

I never would have been as bold as Geronimo. To go down into the basement while our father was there and ask him to explain it to me. He was so solitary, and we were so many that I found it hard to imagine he would have time for me.

I would tremble with emotion if he happened to lay his hand on my shoulder. So imagining that he might have a private conversation with me ...

Besides, I had an unpleasant memory of the only time I had been alone with our father. Alone is relative, of course. There were about fifteen of us there at the time. It was my birthday. I was turning seven, the age of reason, the age when our father introduced us to dynamite.

There were the Weewuns, the Twins, and then Tintin, El Toro, Big Yellow, Zorro, Mustang – anyone the Big Kids had called the Middle Kids and who, since they had left, had become the Big Kids for the Little Kids, the Weewuns. The Old Maid was one of them. Geronimo too. They still lived at home, which was unusual for their age, particularly the Old Maid who, if I do the math, was twenty-three years old and who, rather than having a husband and two or three rug rats, stood in for our mother, our real mother being too busy with her pots and pans, too busy, in fact, to be at the ceremony. And, of course, there was our father.

He initiated his children to dynamite at the sand quarry. The festivities began as soon as we left the house. We would pile into our father's van, an old 1950s Ford, and since it was already filled with all of his drill steels, pickaxes, shovels and bags of rocks, we couldn't all fit, so it was a question of who would have the honour of travelling on the hood, on the back bumper or hanging on to the door, one foot on the running board and the other left dangling to heighten the pleasure. We would shout ourselves hoarse the whole way, singing and chanting lord knows what, our father joining in on the racket with the horn, a rare and delicious moment in our family life when he would wake from his reverie and join us in our brazenness.

I was seated to his right, a place of honour reserved for me because of the day, and my heart was seized with worry. I wasn't afraid of the dynamite, really; it was the long, close contact with our father with the others looking on that scared me.

I was familiar with the ritual. It was repeated for each of our birthdays. Fall offered the most opportunities for blasting because of the birthdays of Tootsie, Mustang, Wapiti and the Twins, but there were only two in the winter (my favourites: the geyser of snow that fell back to the ground in a glittering spray was pure magic), and mine would come with the thaw, just before the festival of cats.

I knew how to handle dynamite; we all did, even without having been introduced to it and without having seen it up close. Our father made an imaginary circle with his arm that pushed us back about ten feet, leaving the inside of the circle to him and the initiate, so that we would see only their backs bent over the details of the operation. It was afterwards, back at home, that we learned – it was the initiate's duty to explain everything: how they had punctured the stick and spliced the blasting cap, chose the length of fuse and, then, the most delicate and terrifying part of the operation, how they had managed to push the cap into the end so as to protect the fuse line. But of our father's murmuring, what he had said as their bodies brushed against one another in the middle of the magic circle, the initiate said nothing. Everyone kept that private conversation to themselves. It was a birthday gift.

I will always remember the first words my father spoke to me in the circle.

'Are you scared?'

He was smiling his little half smile, and I, too young to recognize male bonding, thought I had to be a man and answer no.

'You should be. If you're not scared of dynamite, you're a dead man. I'm still more scared of dynamite than I am of lawyers. Many a time it's saved my life. Fear is important.'

Fear. The fear of finding yourself on a rock outcrop when lightning strikes. The fear of selling your shares in a mine too soon. The fear of a fuse that has absorbed humidity. Prudent fear, mistrustful fear, intuitive fear. 'Fear is important. You have to listen to it.' He confided his fears in me to help me overcome my own.

I should have felt reassured, but it was the first time I had to sustain a conversation with our father. At that moment, he became *my* father, mine, and it was too great an honour for a boy of seven. I was simultaneously puffed up with pride and paralyzed with humility, tangled up in my emotions and my words, and suddenly I know longer knew what a cartridge, a blasting cap or a fuse was. His patience was endless; he repeated his explanations, replayed his gestures, always with these words of advice: 'Take your time. If there's one thing dynamite hates, it's haste, and humidity, and a shock. Dynamite is skittish. You need to take precautions.' And I discovered the smell of his breath, the texture of his skin, the feel of his calloused hands and his gentle presence.

I think I got through it without incident, except for the fuse. It had to be cut on a bias, and I trimmed it nice and straight and clean. It was the last thing to be done before lighting it, and I was distracted by everyone looking at us.

My blast wasn't the most spectacular. Too much frozen aggregate combined with loose material. From the row of spruce trees where we had all taken cover, you could see the sand fly up amid chunks that fell in a splash of blackened snow. It was disorderly, jumbled, a bit clownish. Nothing like summer or winter blasts, which sent huge petals shooting up from the ground, superbly and distinctly outlined, forming a cloud in the sky, coming back down in a light drizzle.

And then, when the blast had finished echoing through the silence of the forest, my father struck up my birthday song, *Happy birthday to you*, his fluty voice getting lost amid the others who sang in a chorus *Happy birthday to you, happy birthday, dear Denis*. Our father always called us by our given names, ignoring the nicknames we had for each other. I jumped when I heard them sing my first name, which had dropped out of use in our family.

That was my only blast at the sand quarry. After that, there was the accident at the mine, and we stopped dynamiting there.

The story of my initiation to dynamite is a big hit in conversations. People cry: 'Seven years old and he let you play with dynamite!' They protest: 'You're not serious!' They exclaim, they are scandalized, but they ask me again: 'Who planted the stick of dynamite in the sand, you or your father?' Particularly the women, the ones with two or three kids, and the busybody mothers who want to hide their disapproval and think they are being subtle: 'And what did your mother think about all this?'

Our mother didn't have time. She would prepare a birthday meal, and we barely saw her behind her enormous table, the fatigue of an entire life making her invisible. But the absent figure of our mother offends these ladies; they don't understand, so I always tell them that she left us to it, which is pretty much true.

There are plenty of parts of our story that I can't tell. People are too narrow-minded to accept such a lust for life. We don't belong to the same species. We never wanted their lives, and I can see in their eyes that our defiance sends them scurrying back to their doghouses with their tails between their legs the minute a particularly Cardinal episode comes up. Over the years, I have figured out which things are the most remarkable, and I don't pour it on any thicker. I stick close to what's deemed acceptable.

I don't tell the story of Geronimo with the stick of dynamite against his chest. I don't want to see – as I have seen reflected in their sidelong, sticky eyes – Geronimo, savage and cruel, standing in front of the school bus that took the hicks back to Hurault, challenging that girl (her name was Caroline) by stroking the tip of the fuse on the stick of dynamite that was jutting out of his windbreaker pocket.

He was in love with another girl, and this Caroline had been ruining it by telling anyone who would listen for the previous three days that he had tried to kiss her. He was twelve years old, already savvy with dynamite, but not so savvy in love, and he was miserable.

Geronimo wasn't the horrible bloodthirsty beast that I can see reflected in their pathetic mongrel eyes. He just wanted to get that hick Caroline to admit she had lied. And he would have gone back, day after day, in front of the Hurault bus, with his stick of dynamite conspicuously hidden in the pocket of his windbreaker, if the story hadn't reached our principal's ears. She summoned Geronimo to her office, along with the schoolyard monitor who, by unhappy coincidence, was the Old Maid. She made it clear to both of them that a monitor couldn't tolerate such conduct.

Geronimo would never have given in, and the principal knew it, if the Old Maid's job hadn't been at stake.

'My job as a schoolyard monitor meant more to me than anything. Geronimo knew it. I used the money from my shifts to buy clothes, and I helped the Old Lady out when she was short for groceries. You know how proud she was of her cooking.'

The Old Maid told me a lot more of this story than she had meant to, during one of our conversations about what our family had been. But she never revealed the name of the girl who had stolen Geronimo's heart. She wasn't even pretty, but she had the beauty of the devil deep in her eyes. That was all I could drag out of her.

Would he have done it? That was a question she wouldn't answer, and to distract me from the stick of dynamite, she told me about things I hadn't asked about.

He would have done it, although what, exactly, I don't think even he knew.

A young warrior – that's how I picture him – a young warrior who didn't know where to thrust his sword, but who was valiantly determined to have his love story.

The Old Maid smiled at the image.

'Except that time, the young warrior didn't win the duel for love. His beloved left Norco a little while later. Her father found work, somewhere else of course, and the family followed.'

The Old Maid is our second mother. She took care of us from the cradle and continues to watch over us. We are at either ends of the family spectrum. Her at the front of the line, the eldest girl, and me at the back. Time could have separated us even more, but whenever my work takes me to Val-d'Or, we meet at the Tim Hortons over a coffee and two doughnuts, and we continue our family odyssey, me a fan in the front row and her trying her hardest not to enjoy it.

I sense her resistance, a knot that tightens and keeps me from traipsing wherever I like. She keeps me on a leash; I can feel it. I can't go farther than her reticence and silence will allow. There is a secret place that she keeps me away from with all her might.

We are always happy to see each other, though. It is incredibly and joyously invigorating, the pleasure of being among Cardinals again. We get so few opportunities. Life has scattered us around the globe.

Émilien is in Australia. He's done a bunch of different jobs that have made him rich. He is the eldest, the Patriarch, as he was once called. We also called him Stan, Stanley and Siscoe, because of an old story about Stanley Siscoe's wad of cash. But none of the nicknames we gave him stuck: he was too remote, too old, practically an uncle.

Big Yellow is fighting fascism, imperialism, injustice and all of that in South America. I last saw him five years ago. He was on his way to Frankfurt, supposedly for a conference on international aid. I didn't believe him. I think he's an arms dealer. That's what the Old Maid thinks too.

Mustang has been on the move since his first divorce, Tommy is lying low somewhere in Ungava, Nefertiti exists only by cellphone and there is no point trying to get Tintin to leave behind his life of poverty. We see each other in groups of two or three, never all at once. We haven't had a family reunion since Norco.

So when I saw everyone walk into the lobby of the Quatre-Temps one after the other, I thought this was it, our family reunion, the great Cardinal celebration I had spent thirty years hoping for.

The Quatre-Temps is a long, depressing building with tentacles that reach out into the spruce forest at the southern limit of Val-d'Or. Inside, it's all fake leather, fake oak and fake smiles. It tries to create the illusion of a luxury hotel. This is where the prospectors' conference is held every year, in this labyrinth of corridors and illusion. This is where, I hope, the wonder that is my family will be returned to me.

They all came. I don't know how the word got around. The Old Maid was the one who had told me about it. Last month, at the Tim Hortons. In fact it was the first thing she said, she was so excited.

'Prospector Emeritus? They're going to give him the Prospector of the Year medal?'

I didn't understand. Our father was still prospecting, of course, but at eighty-one years old, he wasn't what he once was. When I visit him in his little bungalow (an abomination, I still can't get used to it) and I go down to his finished basement (another abomination) where, inevitably, I find him gripping his cane but busy with his maps, books and rock samples brought from Norco, he is, and to my eyes shall remain, the only truly great prospector in the world. Even though he is no longer out in the field, even though he has swapped pickaxe and compass for the phone, even in slippers and a wool cardigan in his chilly basement, he is still the man we would see coming home from his claims, late in the evening, with the smell of the forest on him, a tired silence and, in his eyes, the metallic glint of the vein waiting for him in the bowels of the earth.

But Prospector Emeritus for 1995? I still don't understand. He hasn't discovered anything important since 1944, since the zinc deposit that Northern Consolidated deftly stole from him.

And I don't understand what happened to us at the prospectors' conference either.

I arrived in the Quatre-Temps lobby before the others. I wanted to watch them walk in. Most of all, I wanted to see who would come. I had passed along the news to many of them, hoping they would spread the word, but I never thought it would make it around the world.

I hadn't seen some of them since Norco. Geronimo, for instance. After Norco, he went back to school and hadn't wavered from his goal. He got his doctorate in medicine, specializing in vascular surgery and orthopedics, all from a Grade 9 education, and by age thirty-nine he had embarked on an illustrious career as a war surgeon. Chad, Ethiopia, Chechnya: he had been to all the world's hot spots. A latter-day Bethune of sorts. He had never taken out tonsils. I saw him on TV a few years ago being interviewed about Afghanistan. The jet black hair, the ashen complexion, the eye of a jaguar – I would have recognized him anywhere. He was pure Cardinal.

I didn't recognize the Twins. They had faded with time. Carmelle and Angèle. Tommy and the Twin, as we called them. Tommy, because she could strike a trout like nobody's business, because she was our best right winger in hockey and our pride and joy in jiu-jitsu, a real tomboy, the neighbours liked to say. And to show them we couldn't care less what they thought and that she belonged to us, we called her Tommy. The Twin? Because … there were so many of us, some just went unnoticed.

They had aged from the inside. They had curdled, withdrawn. They were impenetrable. They could have been any woman nearing fifty. I hadn't seen them since Norco, and it took El Toro saying, 'Hey, there's Tommy,' before I could pick out which gloomy, sullen woman was my sister.

To see one was to see the other, they looked so much alike. But I didn't see them together once during the conference. It was as if they were avoiding each other.

As soon as the conference started, it felt as though my family was slipping through my fingers. Already, in the lobby, as they arrived one after the other, Cardinals gathering near the front desk, I felt an edginess, a desire to slip away. I saw Big Yellow and Yahoo sneak off to their rooms.

The uneasiness grew as more of them arrived. There was the joy of seeing each other again, of course, the outpouring of cries and thumps on the back, happy reunions, as I had hoped. But the eyes of each new arrival showed a flash of panic as our numbers grew near the front desk. Between the cries and back thumps, some deserted, going off to their rooms, and others slipped away to the bar or the restaurant. There were only five of us left at the front desk when our parents made their entrance.

It was like chasing shadows that won't stand still. I went from one to the other, running, searching, but the shadows slipped away, the groups broke up, and I would find myself alone with an interrupted conversation, my heart in my hands.

It was as if we were repelling each other. As if, above the Quatre-Temps, a giant, crazed magnet were playing with us. As if, after all these years, we couldn't stand to be together.

There was a moment of grace that broke the evil spell. An incredible image that no one could resist, a moment when we were all drawn to an extraordinary scene, at the centre of the Quatre-Temps exhibition hall. Our father, in front of a state-of-the-art computer, talking about cross-referencing geographical data and satellite images with the young technician, was translating the short young man's coded language for two prospector friends seated beside him, who were chewing on their astonishment. It was a thing to behold.

I heard El Toro say behind me, 'He's never touched a computer in his life!'

We were shocked and amazed.

The diminutive technician, who was just as dumbfounded, was offering explanations and giving instructions, and our father was executing them, his awkward fingers stumbling over the keyboard, as what they had agreed upon appeared on the screen. A prodigy, a genius as he headed to the other exhibition booths, trailing a crowd of curious onlookers behind him.

I was in the front row, between Big Yellow and Magnum. Behind us, beside El Toro, was the Old Maid. I heard her offer by way of explanation, 'He learned from books. You should see all the computer books he has in his basement.'

Wapiti, a bit further back, begged to differ.

'That's cutting-edge technology. He couldn't have learned that from books.'

I hadn't yet realized that we were all there.

Our semi-circle around the computer grew smaller under the crush of the crowd. At one point, I was ejected from the arc and pushed against the chair of one of the old prospectors, the old coot with the nicotine-stained teeth. He leaned in toward our father and said, 'Albert, you have company.'

Our father, eyes wide from the strain of looking at the screen, turned to us. I followed his eyes and realized that the family had gathered around him.

I had recognized the other old prospector right away. He used to come to Norco from time to time. I recognized the scar among the folds of his skin. 'A mother bear defending her cubs,' he had told us when, as kids, we climbed on him to plunge our fingers into the purplish gash of the wound. But he wasn't sure whether he recognized us.

'They're your kids? All of them? Yours?'

Senility, no doubt. How could he not recognize us?

That's when the old coot with the nicotine-stained teeth asked the question that would bring the conversation around to my favourite topic.

'That's quite a herd you have there. Just how many are there, Albert?'

I was waiting for the answer. I was waiting for the magic number that would stupefy and amaze. We would dazzle them with our stories. Finally we would all be together again, reunited in the spotlight of our memories.

I waited for the answer to echo through the crowd.

'Twenty-one. Twenty-one children.'

But among us, in the semi-circle around our father, there was nothing. Dead silence.

The old coot with the nicotine-stained teeth followed up with another question.

'Twenty-one, and they're all living?'

The silence turned to pain. A pain that stabbed at me and united us – me, who didn't understand what was going on, and them, frozen as the seconds ticked by, waiting to hear what our father would say.

'Twenty-one, and all living.'

Our father's eyes froze, blank. I turned around. My brothers, my sisters, my mother. Blank stares, all of them.

The Caboose looked at us one after the other, then all at once, and my stomach lurched. I'd thought he had figured it out. At the Tim Hortons, when I feel like he's on the verge of illuminating part of the shadow, like he's going to put his finger on it, grab on to my silence and be pulled through the curtain, I distract him. I tell him about Geronimo, I tell him about Tintin, I tell him about Norco, the long grass, the vast blue desolation of the winters, our house, the madness of our evenings, our dreams, our freedom, which is more than he has asked for, and he forgets the shadow that rose up. But there, at the Quatre-Temps, in the crush of the conference, I was trapped. I couldn't stop what was happening.

It was old Savard who saved us. Old Scarface. The Weewuns loved him. They would climb his great, grubby carcass, plunge their fingers into the furrowed flesh and, every time, ask him how he got the scar. He was already old at the time, and he reeked like a man ravaged by years spent roaming the forests and the grimy hotels of Val-d'Or. He would hang around the kitchen, teasing the Old Lady and me with shameless vulgarity, the only civilities he was capable of in the presence of women. I would have chased him out with a broom if he hadn't been there for our father. And I could have kissed him when he offered us an out.

The silence was thick, and we couldn't react when old Savard, suddenly realizing he recognized us, pointed at Geronimo and asked our father:

'That's little Laurent, the one who used to follow you every-where. Did any of the others go rock crazy?'

The people around us laughed, because little Laurent is almost six feet tall. Because the expression *rock crazy* is an archaic one, and it landed like a fossilized joke among the young geologists assembled. Because everyone had felt the weight of the silence.

We laughed too. Though it took us a few seconds to get the laugh going, having been paralyzed.

It had all gone over the Caboose's head. I was sure of it when I saw him take an interest in the conversation. There was no shadow in his eyes. On the contrary, he was elated, our Caboose, convinced that old Savard was going to take us back to his memories of us when he used to come to get the latest on our father's dreams and when he let the Weewuns slide down his long legs.

'Laurent is more interested in bones than rocks now. He's a doctor. Patching 'em up in Chechnya. He's a surgeon.'

'You would have done better if you'd had a lawyer. You'd be rich right now if you had a lawyer for a son.'

'Ugh! Not a lawyer! But one of my sons went rock crazy. He had a claim in Fancamp township with Lachapelle last year. And then there's my oldest, Émilien, who's sampling rock in Australia. That's hardly a stone's throw.'

Savard kept needling our father who, never having understood sarcasm, let himself be carried along by his old friend's teasing. People were laughing kindly. The conversation had taken a reassuring turn. I was breathing more easily.

I took a quick look around me. Tintin had disappeared. I saw Nefertiti slip out quietly, and I met Tut's eye, which assured me that he would do the same. Quietly, carefully, we beat a retreat, and if anyone had decided to do a count, they wouldn't have known to go off in search of the twenty-first.

The Caboose was so absorbed by what the three old men were saying that he didn't see anything. He is insatiable when it comes to stories of our family. The old-timers were reminiscing about a trench they had cut into hard quartz. Smoky quartz, gleaming black: that detail came from our father. It had been a long way from Norco, light years from our family history. But it was about mines – incredible, rich, gigantic – hidden in the rock, waiting to be discovered, so our father was talkative, with his soft, singsong voice that used to startle us at the table, so rarely was it heard. It was more than enough to make the Caboose's day.

He is insatiable. Sometimes if I'm not on my guard, I find myself swept up in memories I haven't erased – how could I? – that are buried in the back of my brain. All it takes is the slightest thing. All it takes is for the Caboose to show a little too much interest in a detail, and the conversation brushes back up against the shadow I have skirted.

I hadn't wanted to tell Geronimo's love story. It had a courtly beauty – the Caboose had described it that way – but was unbearably painful, the same type of pain that has plagued our hearts since Angèle disappeared. We have a gift for pain. And when I think back to Geronimo's heartbreak, I poke around in the hurt that has disfigured us all so horribly. Pain begets pain, and the Caboose, who has been spared, sees in that story only the beauty of the gesture.

I never told him about Geronimo's fever and horrible migraine. He had never been sick, not even a winter flu, and when I saw him clench his teeth in pain in the principal's office, I thought he was furious at his powerlessness. He's tough, our Geronimo. He can hold back more than his weight in tears. Even at age twelve, when that little girl broke his heart, it was clear that he would be an important figure in our family story.

He didn't unclench his teeth. The principal, despite the authority of her padded chair, her enormous bosom and her principal's doublespeak, couldn't get a word out of him. He was gripping his chair, his hands like talons, his arms tensed, his neck sunk into his torso, a young wildcat observing something bigger than him and biding his time.

This was not their first confrontation. Geronimo was the king of the schoolyard, which regularly landed him in the principal's office, rightly or wrongly. But I'd never had to answer for the things he did. We were both monitors, and he stayed away from my area.

The school bus loading zone wasn't my responsibility that day. We all knew that, the principal, Geronimo and me. That only made the threat more treacherous when she said, from above her imposing bosom, 'But you must realize that a monitor can't allow children to be walking around the schoolyard with sticks of dynamite.'

I thought he was going to throw himself at her and maul her enormous boobs. He jumped from his chair with all the ferocity he could muster and – this is Geronimo's particular brand of intelligence – without hesitating, he brought his hand gently from the pocket of his windbreaker, removing the offending object, which he pretended to offer to the principal.

Inside, I was jumping for joy. She had probably never seen dynamite in her life. Her enormous boobs quivered in unison, in fear or indignation. She wanted to get up, take charge of the situation, but Geronimo hadn't budged, hadn't withdrawn the authority of the stick of dynamite by so much as a millimetre, and the principal sunk into the great expanse of her trembling flesh, the chair yielding under the shock with a soft hiss.

That's where the story ends. I don't tell the rest. It's what I give the Caboose when he brings the conversation around to what has become, in our family, 'the time Geronimo made the principal's boobs shake.' The story is part of our heritage. That story, and many others, made for enjoyable evenings. We have an endless repertoire of stories and, at night, after the battles over the dishes and the battles for the three-seater sofa, the kids would settle in any which way they could in front of the television, and, from the living room doorway, I would listen to them. My workday wasn't finished yet, but I couldn't help but be there, in the centre of the house, propped up against the doorframe, one foot in the kitchen and the other in the living room, listening to what they had to say about their exploits at school, about tv, about the world that was opening up to them, about what they would do to all the hicks of the world once they left Norco.

I never managed to finish my day's work, the house stayed messy and our evenings are some of my happiest memories.

The house would be lit up like a cathedral. There would be someone in every room and someone moving between them, but the epicentre of our chaotic evenings was the living room, specifically the hollow of the sofa, where the victors had managed to take their place after the battle over dishes – generally Geronimo, Tintin and Tommy, although often Tommy couldn't hold her own against Matma. The others, those who perched on the arms or on the back, were the keepers of the sofa. There were three, four, sometimes five of them – the Weewuns, inevitably, since the old ones were too proud and their legs too long – and once one of the overlords of the sofa got up for a glass of water or milk, or to empty it all into the wc, the keepers battled for the privilege of saving that person's place. Sometimes – and herein lay the fun of the game – the Weewuns weren't fast enough or wasted too much time squabbling, and a seat stealer would sneak onto the sofa. The overlord would come back, chew out both the keepers and the thief, and join the seatless, grumbling, stretched out on the ground or crouched in a corner, keeping an eye on the queue-jumper in case he went to get a drink or have a pee, such that the battle for the sofa continued all evening long.

However, there was a magic word, a word that had the force of law and took the harsh edge off the game. Otherwise, there would have been even more fists flying. I don't remember when it became part of the game. 'What does it matter?' Yahoo said when I asked him. 'It stuck, and it made us laugh.' The word originally was a sentence, a clearly issued warning: *That's my place* or some such thing. With time and repeated use, the sentence had become *Smyplace*.

Smyplace, and the overlord could go to the kitchen or the wc in peace, the right of ownership established. But there was always someone to steal the place. And depending on the mood that reigned that evening, it was settled by argument or a rip-roaring fight. For fun or for real.

The word was used for a lot of things other than the battle for the sofa. *Smyplace* for a chair, for a shady corner of the porch, *smy* for anything we wanted to designate as personal property and that, necessarily, was the object of a power struggle. The same code of honour, the same swindling and the same fights.

It became *Smyshirt, Smyboots, Smypen, Smyrifle, SmyCornflakes* – a fairly tenuous way of preserving a right of ownership in a house where nothing, absolutely nothing, not even a place to sleep, was personally assigned to us. We slept in whatever bed was free, and we put on whatever we found among the clothes piled in what I called my laundry room, which had been the kitchen/living room of one of the units of this incredible house that had had four of them at the start.

We were most fierce about protecting the clothes. But, often, *Smysweater* wasn't enough. You had to sleep in whatever you wanted to wear the next day. The morning fights weren't as violent among the girls – there were only five of us – but it was like Armageddon if the boys had decided, in an effort to provoke or out of pure maliciousness, that their hearts were set on the same article of clothing.

We lived in the most wonderful anarchy, and I loved that house. The doors slammed, the stairs trembled, the walls shook, life stamped its feet with impatience in that house, and I was its caretaker. I was the one who swept, shovelled, washed and bleached, who every morning dove into endless piles of laundry, who chased dust bunnies and the mess in bedrooms, only ever managing to move them around. I was the one who reigned over the disorder.

The four units made for a magnificently quirky abode, a maze of doors and kitchen/living rooms that suited our disorganized lives to a T. I have loved disorder ever since. My children, and particularly my husbands, didn't. They all left.

My realm was upstairs, in the west kitchen/living room, in what was the laundry room and what Geronimo called the rag room.

Where's the Old Maid?
The Old Maid is in the rag room.
Why is the Old Maid in there?
Because the Old Maid is on the rag.

There was no authority figure in the house, and this little verse, which I was constantly serenaded with, served to remind me that doing the wash didn't make me one.

So we piled our clothes in the laundry room. The dirty and the clean. The dirty were heaped in a mountain around the washing machine. And the clean were stacked in our father's dynamite boxes, some washed and brushed out, others still grey with dried mud, which served as chests of drawers and were piled along the walls. All of this happily intermingled. I washed the clean and the dirty without distinction, and at noon, whether I was finished or not, I moved on to something else.

In another kitchen/living room there was a table, a few chairs, a rocking chair and an impressive number of books. The table was actually a door set on trestles, a door ripped from an abandoned house that my siblings then diligently and enthusiastically damaged so they would have to go get another one. The books, on the other hand, were carefully put away in a white pine bookshelf.

This was the study, the place where the Cardinals engaged in book learning, the place where the worlds of science, the arts and power were theirs to conquer, the place where the loftiest of ambitions seemed possible.

That was where I heard Zorro dream of becoming an engineer. I think he just liked the sound of the word, because when Tintin asked him, it turned out he had no idea what an engineer did. It took him several days – and the dictionary, I'm sure – to finally answer, 'An engineer builds military machines.'

Then he wanted to be an architect, and then a sculptor, a painter, a poet, finally admitting, one fine evening, that he would be nothing less than a modern-day Leonardo da Vinci. The dictionary had served him once again.

'And what about being a fag, too?'

I don't know where Matma picked that up, but one thing was sure, he got the fight he was looking for. He wanted to be an inventor too, and having his dream stolen by a war engineer, even Leonardo da Vinci, was more than he could take. He had been nicknamed Matma – for Gandhi, the great apostle of non-violence. It was ironic, of course, because there was little tolerance in the highly charged genes of our Mahatma.

In spite of it all, the study was the calmest place in the house, and that's where I rocked the babies.

'That's where you played dolly.'

Untrue, patently untrue. The swaddled little bundles that landed in my arms just a few days after their birth were like my own children. They smelled of milk, fresh cotton and the gentle things in life. Little, pink, downy balls, tender and warm in the crook of my arm. They were my little ones, and I was their mother. And they all came back to me at some point to hear about their childhood. *How old was I when I started walking? Is it*

true that I couldn't tolerate milk? You gave me pieces of meat to suckle!
They would ask about the others, compare themselves to them,
recreate their memories. *Did the Caboose really have a pointy head?*
I walked at ten and a half months? Before Wapiti? Before Geronimo!
They were amused by the shortcomings of the others, amused
by what they didn't know about their own childhood, amused
by their big sister playing dolly – no, I wasn't playing dolly –
but deep down we are all after the same thing. We all want to
go back to Norco, back to the hustle of our lives, to understand
what we were, what we have become and, most importantly, we
want to solve the riddle of our parents. Our father, a pale version
of what he was deep down and never let us see, enslaved by his
obsession with rocks. Our mother, there, always in the kitchen,
lost in the clatter of pots and steam, and who, because she was
always there, was invisible.

I'm the one who gets the questions. They think being the
oldest means that I was in on the secrets.

'All those years of taking care of the babies and the house,
and she didn't tell you anything?'

I wasn't even six the first time she gave me a baby to rock. It
was Angèle, the Twin, Angèle who was so cruelly taken from
us and whom I took from my mother's trembling arms.

'Take the baby, there's a big girl. The other one is burning
up with fever.'

The other one was Tommy, of course, and they had to be
separated because of the fever, because of the terrible illness that
it heralded and that could have taken both babies to their grave.

'I haven't lost a single one.'

My mother's triumph, her greatest fear, and the only time
she ever confided in me.

I rocked every baby after that. She would bring them to me,
still warm and smelling of her bed, and she would go back to
the kitchen.

During the few days when she would withdraw to her room, the house held its breath. No more racing up and down the stairs, no more sofa wars, no more punching or arguing. Our mother was having another baby. The house drifted along in a surreal state, and the kitchen, without her, without the worn-down and bewildered presence of our mother, lay dying.

I think that when our mother was alone in her bedroom with the baby, with the door closed, she pined to be with us, in the heart of the house, in the kitchen, simmering her enormous stews. Once a rush of vitality came back to her, she would leave her bedroom, her eyes frantic and her step unsteady, hand the baby over to me, and get back to her pots.

'I think she missed the kitchen.'

The Caboose started when I told him that. It shocked him, I think. He would rather I keep talking about babies.

'And did she rock me?'

No, dear Caboose, she didn't rock you. She was already close to the edge, and she didn't have time, even though after you there were no more babies kicking in her belly.

She was driven by urgency: the urgency of meals, the urgency of children, the urgency of the days going by, the urgency of thoughts that she chased off with confused mumbling ... I don't know why she was in such a rush. She was always out of breath. She went back and forth in great strides, as if she had kilometres to travel between the sink and the stove. Terrorized by time, sighing, labouring like a madwoman, muttering like a kook. And if one of us had something to ask her, we had to repeat it several times so that, finally plucked from the muddle of her thoughts, she would lift her head, surprised and lost: 'What?' We barely had time to explain, and she would already have forgotten, sighing with an absent voice, 'I don't know. Go ask Émilienne, she knows.' I couldn't stand it. Every time, it took all the humility I had to quell my anger and say, 'Mother, I'm Émilienne.'

– 34 –

'So what was she muttering about all the time?'

At the time, I thought I was the only one who wondered about our mother's compulsive muttering. Everyone in the house was busy dreaming about their lives. I was the only one truly there. That's what I thought until years later when I was asked about the ritual of meals, our mother's nightly rounds and the incessant muttering.

'Recipes, she was reciting recipes. So she wouldn't forget them.'

Recipes, yes, I heard them too, but there was more than an obsession with meals in the drone of her thoughts. I don't know how many times I heard her chanting a recipe, and then, all of a sudden, struck by inspiration, she would freeze, her eyes dark with worry, her breath trapped by a painful thought, and finally, after a seemingly endless wait, a long, heavy exhale would escape her and then, in the hoarse hissing of a voice that was not her own, I would hear a name escape her lips, the name of one of her children. One of us had just flapped our wings against the walls of her panicked memory.

How can I explain …

She loved us. You just had to see the tenderness, the gentle looks, the love she swaddled her babies in before entrusting them to me. But her tender passion was nothing against the panic that drove her into the kitchen. She forgot the baby, she forgot all of us, one by one, because of the panicked love she had for all her children, and if one of us popped into her thoughts, alone and singled out in the jumble of faces of children that got tangled up in her mind, it was panic; she just realized she had forgotten that child.

But she had found a way to overcome her confusion. When we were at the table, she counted us. Each person had an assigned place – there was to be no bickering here, and *Smyplace* didn't work – and, while we were serving ourselves, her eyes moved to each one of us to make sure we were all there. It was a delicious moment.

'I wouldn't have missed that moment for the world. I would stare at the plate and wait for her eyes to land on me. It was like a prayer.'

Tootsie is the second to last, the youngest girl, just before the Caboose, and she has her own way of expressing things.

Our mother counted us, one by one, and when she had gathered everyone who made up her world in her line of sight, she would turn back to the counter where urgent matters still awaited. She never sat down. No time, not hungry, she tasted this and that, feeding herself with the ladle or the spatula. It was only after the evening meal, after making sure everything was set for the next morning's meal, that she allowed herself to rest and withdraw to her room.

If the Caboose had counted us in our semi-circle around the computer, properly counted us, one by one, like our mother had, he would have realized.

We had done everything possible to avoid being all together at one time since Angèle disappeared. There were no more family gatherings. It was an unwritten rule. Our mother mustn't realize that she was missing a child. We didn't take the same precautions with our father. He knows. The way he clams up whenever Angèle's memory skims the surface of the conversation, we know he knows.

There is something about our mother that asks to be protected. A rip, a deep gash that her mind gets lost in. Sometimes I watch her huffing and puffing in the kitchen of her bungalow as if she still has a brood to feed, and I wonder what makes her want to lose herself like that. She is seventy-eight years old, her joints are eaten away by arthritis, her heart menaced by her arteries, and still she toils away like a forced labourer. The charities gobble up the meals by the potful.

When we get together, in twos, threes or fours, rarely more, our first question, inevitably, is about her: 'How is the Old Lady?'

We want to protect her, to cup her in the palm of our hand, but she always gets away. She takes off ahead of herself and leaves us with a blurry image we have never stopped wondering about. An elusive creature, who, in our minds, really only existed at night when she appeared at the bed we were sleeping in, her long hair hanging loose, her bony silhouette softened by the filmy contours of her nightgown and the rosy glow of the tiny flashlight that accompanied her on her nightly rounds, which she turned toward the palm of her hand so as not to wake us when she approached.

The fleeting image of our mother has haunted our nights and followed us throughout our lives. I still find myself waiting for her, alone in the bed of the little room at the hotel where I work my fingers to the bone in the kitchen six days a week. The room is as rundown as the one I had in Norco. I imagine that I hear the floor creak gently under her step, I curl up under the covers and she arrives at my door, opens it noiselessly – I wonder if I should hold my breath – then moves toward the chair beside my bed and sits down on the pile of clothes. Then the moment I love so much arrives, the one when she looks at me, me, Émili-enne, her eldest girl. I am eight years old, fifteen, twenty-one, fifty-three, and she looks at me, her child.

Sometimes she would nod off in the chair and stay there sleeping for a long time. I would have pins and needles all over my body from staying in the same position so long to watch her. The best, but the most uncomfortable, was lying on my back. That way I could get a peek at her and, sometimes, fall asleep contemplating the image of my mother.

She had a gentleness, a grace that was so inviting that it was like being visited by an angel. All the hardness of her features, all the worries that showed on her face, all the day's difficulties vanished and she rested, at peace, a thin smile on her lips, her head bowed slightly, her long hair haloed by the brightness of the moon, a Madonna, and all around her body, the matte soft-ness of the light she kept in the palm of her hand and that spread over her nightgown.

'A Madonna. I couldn't sleep until she appeared.'

We all have, tucked deep in our hearts, an image of our mother's nighttime apparitions that haunts our lives.

She went from room to room, her little flashlight guiding her steps. It was past midnight when she started her rounds. Everyone was in bed, there was no one left in front of the tele-vision, the evening's mayhem had subsided. I would hear her close her bedroom door behind her. Softly, without making too much noise. The house had aches and pains throughout, and in spite of her precautions, my mother couldn't stop the creaking, groaning and squeaking that accompanied her on her rounds and told us where she was.

Because of the babies who slept with me, I was the only one who had a bedroom – upstairs, just above our mother's – and I think it was because of the babies that her rounds began in my room. All the others slept wherever they could find space, the only rule being that the girls and the boys didn't sleep together, and sometimes someone would spend the night on the sofa in the living room or on a pile of clothes in the laundry room.

I would hear our mother climb the ladder that led to the second floor through a hole in the kitchen ceiling. The ladder was very steep and shaky, having been built a long time before by our father's clumsy hands and patched up by one of us when a rung went missing or an upright was about to give way. A staircase would have been more practical, but it was beyond our father's skills once he had realized, in moving his family into the house, that there had to be a means for moving between the two floors indoors. Maybe he had thought about our mother in her nightgown, in the snow, wind and cold that an outdoor staircase would have exposed her to. Never mind that the groaning of the ladder in the silence of the house made me worry every time that she would get caught up in her long night-gown and lose her footing.

Nights with a full moon were a blessing. I could take my time studying her as she dozed at the foot of my bed.

Big Yellow just thought she was an insomniac. 'It was only while she watched us sleep that her own sleep could creep up and she would manage to outsmart the insomnia a little.'

I think that her nights were in fact states of intense alertness. She emerged from the whirlwind of her days, made serene by her evening rest, and made the rounds of the beds to see each of her children, as they were when she gave birth to them, restored to her in sleep, relaxed, peaceful and innocent, and she wanted to store that in her memory forever.

What makes me think this is her gentle, loving gaze, which went to the far reaches of my soul, and the incredible emptiness I felt when her eyes moved to one of the little ones sleeping with me.

What makes me think this is what Yahoo told me and what Zorro and Nefertiti confirmed. They had run into her one time on their way to the bathroom.

'I was coming out of the wc,' Yahoo told me. 'It was a clear, cold winter night, a full moon. The temperature had dipped below minus forty.

'She was coming out of the green bedroom. Do you remember the green bedroom? Fakir had picked the colour, that time we repainted the house.

'I was hurrying, because the cold was burning my feet, and I stopped short when I saw her. She looked like someone out for a stroll. She was barefoot but didn't seem to feel the cold. She leaned toward me – I was eight or nine – and she said, 'Get back to bed, Julien. You're going to catch cold. The floor is like ice.'

'She was tall and beautiful in the moonlight. She had a soft, calm voice.

'I was so surprised to see her, and particularly to hear her say my name, that I dashed off to the bedroom without saying a word.

'She laughed a little, she thought it was funny – she laughed, can you imagine? – and she said, 'No, Julien, not that one. You're sleeping in the other room.''

What had impressed Yahoo was that she knew where he was sleeping that night.

'Did she operate on radar, or what?'

Bibi, to whom I told the story, had a simpler explanation.

'She counted us. She counted the beds and who was in them, and she knew exactly where each one of us was.'

Yahoo's story supports the image I have of our mother, frantic during the day but mistress of her nights.

I like to think that we shared responsibility for the household. I cared for the brood of Cardinals, big and small, while she cooked obsessively and watched over our nights. The house was safe.

I would like to have the same confidence today. The family is scattered around the world. There are no more discussions, no more battles, no more big dreams to dream. Only the slow drip of pain.

The house is like the family. Battered, disfigured, but holding on. It's the only building still standing in Norco. I go back sometimes, fearing each time that it will have fallen down, but no, it's still standing, collapsing under its own weight, open to the elements, and always there, a noble, faithful companion.

Sometimes, I find it more broken-down, more creaky. Its porches and outdoor staircases have fallen off. It is gaping open on all sides. There are no more doors or windows to protect it. The scalloped trim that gave it its phony facade – the only nod to style – is now home to a colony of birds, barn swallows and starlings that cheep frightfully and scatter when I appear.

Norco is now just a field surrounded by forest. The impression of a wide-open space that I had back then crashes into the trees that have sprouted up everywhere. There are trees in the Laroses' yard, the Boissonneaults' and the Morins', where the church, the Hôtel Impérial and the Decarufel garage were. The only place that has been spared the encroachment is the block where the three schools stood.

I don't recognize the old Norco. Its houses are ruins, its cars mere shells, everything has been flattened under a layer of grass. The forest is preparing its advance, and the mine, hidden away in the mountain that is the town's backdrop, sits there waiting for me to go take a look. But I won't.

I don't know what miracle saved our father's dynamite shed from the devastation. It wasn't even very solid – nothing our father built was ever particularly straight.

It looks like a big spider. The boards – the ones that are still upright – have separated from the base and now offer only diagonal support. The roof, eaten away by rust, has holes in several places.

A big spider with a rusty sheet-metal hood.

It was our father's domain. He stored his dynamite in it, along with all the prospecting equipment he couldn't cart around in his van or pile in the basement. He spent a lot of time in the shed, watched from the window by one of the Weewuns who would announce, 'The Old Man's going to the shed; the Old Man's coming back from the shed.' Our father's comings and goings were always worthy of comment. We saw so little of him.

He could spend weeks in the woods, but when one of his claims was close by, for example in Barraute or Lamorandière township, he came back each night. Which didn't much affect his presence in the house, since he left at the crack of dawn and came back only at suppertime, and as soon as he got up from the table, he headed down to the basement where his rock samples would fill his dreams all evening.

He was in the basement or he was in the shed. Domestic life didn't interest him. As far as I know, he didn't go into any of the bedrooms apart from his own, where he and our mother would cross paths at the end of the evening, she, setting off on her nightly rounds, and he, emerging from underground. The only time I saw him go upstairs was when Geronimo was lovesick for that little girl with the wild eyes.

Geronimo and I had just come home from school. We had left the principal practically catatonic. Geronimo wasn't much better, I realized only on the way home. His eyes had the milky film of fever. I wanted to touch his forehead, but he pushed my hand away: 'Don't touch me. I have a headache.'

When we got home, he ran upstairs using an outside stair-case, and I went in by the kitchen. It was spring, the ground was spewing the last of winter, and the children coming home from school were splashing merrily in the runoff of muddy snow, looking for trickling treasures liberated by the thaw. The only ones at home were the Weewuns and our mother. The Weewuns – Tootsie, Wapiti and Nefertiti, the Caboose hadn't been born yet – were too young to remember, and the Old Lady was in the basement. I'm the only one who saw our father climb the kitchen ladder.

He had come home from his claims earlier than usual. After unloading his equipment in the shed, he came in and asked me where Laurent was. As if he already knew that Geronimo wasn't playing outside with the others, that he was feverish, sick and had gone to bed. As if he had had a premonition.

'He's upstairs. He's running a fever.'

'Headache?'

I nodded with a gesture of impotence. He hesitated a moment, looked at me, really looked, and climbed the ladder.

That moment belongs to me. I never told anyone about it. Just like I never talked about how intimidated our father looked as he went up, his furtive gestures, how embarrassed he was to be intruding in his children's domain.

He stayed upstairs for five long minutes. I counted. When he came down, he was just as uncomfortable.

The Old Lady came up from the basement with a load of potatoes. The Weewuns clung to my legs, and I was never able to explain what had so worried our father, nor the strange impression that this memory leaves every time it surfaces.

I have never told anyone this story, although I have often been tempted. I know it would give me points if they knew that I was the holder of an unfamiliar corner of our father's secret life. It would be fleeting pride, I know, one that would evaporate rather quickly in the disappointment of having destroyed the intimacy of the only moment when my father truly looked at me, when I had the feeling of having an existence all my own.

The one to worry most about is the Caboose. It's hard to resist the pleasure of telling him, seeing such contagious enthusiasm in his eyes for anything involving our family. The Caboose is ardent, he burns, he is consumed with admiration for our life in Norco, which he never knew, the poor thing. He wasn't yet born or was still just a wailing little thing – 'a howling monkey,' Geronimo said – during the best years. Norco was at the start of its decline. The mine had just closed, the streets were emptying, and we felt like just wanting to become rich, powerful, almighty, the masters of the universe was enough. We were champing at the bit in a dying town. Our best years. The late 1950s, the early 1960s.

When we talk about our life in Norco, this is the period we are referring to. Almost all of us were still at home. Only the Big Kids had left. Émilien, Mustang, Yahoo and Fakir were in Montreal, and they would come back, their arms filled with gifts, their old beaters bursting with clothes picked up at manufacturer's surplus sales and, in the trunk, crates of vegetables –

cauliflower, broccoli, mushrooms and other curiosities from the Jean Talon Market, 'Italian food' – that they laid at our mother's feet with the air of conquistadors.

Our best years. The Caboose never gets tired of them. He is constantly looking for an anecdote, a detail, listening for a slight shift in the conversation that will bring us back to that time. When we get together, I know I'll enjoy going back over the memories, but I also know the pain that prowls around the pleasure. The skies went dark at the end of our best years. When we had to leave Norco, the house was completely devastated.

The Caboose experienced the dark years with complete impunity. He was only seven when Angèle disappeared. He didn't know anything about it. The house kept the tragedy in check by holding its breath and coasting on better times.

The Caboose was so fragile. He had no instinct, he was scared of his own shadow. We always protected him. I kept him out of the jaws of the older ones, and they protected him from the hicks. He was the opposite of all we held dear – faint-hearted, indecisive, in fact, he became a civil servant – and yet he was authentically Cardinal in his rejection of what was not absolutely true. He was a paragon of loyalty to our values, without ever having the strength to embody them. He wore our colours. He was kind of our mascot. And during long stretches of boredom, when winter lingered until May or the summer wouldn't let up on the parched land, when Norco's desolation affected us more than usual, the Caboose agreed to be our bait.

They would leave him on his own, seemingly unsupervised. He would play or hang around somewhere and wait for someone to come pick on him. If a hick approached, the band of Cardinals would emerge, judging the severity of the offence by bearing, gestures or tone of voice. If the hick was alone, he got a good scare, but if there was a group, a memorable fight ensued.

These apocalyptic battles made the Caboose the hero of the hour. His siblings carried him home on their shoulders, and he got the glory of telling the story that evening in front of the TV.

Poor Caboose. He never managed to make a place for himself. They were too big, too hard, too sure of their strength, and, being born sickly and pointy headed, he didn't think he measured up. He would run into the fray, scared and cowed by the show of strength, receiving a claw mark on the way, sticking out his tongue and tossing a bad word right back, but he never managed to assert himself.

They tried to toughen him up. They took him everywhere. He was on all the expeditions, but it was a waste of time. He didn't pick up a single ounce of cruelty. He was an onlooker to their games, an onlooker to our life, and we continued to protect him, our gritless Caboose, our scared little Caboose, our most faithful admirer.

He hasn't changed. Still fretful and nervous in his suit and tie. Too frail for us to let him see our pain.

He was the first person Geronimo asked about.

'Is the Caboose here? Has anyone told him? And the Old Lady? How is the Old Lady?'

I knew that the conference would be sort of a reunion when I saw the great Geronimo get out of a rental car in the hotel parking lot. If a phone call had convinced him to leave the war wounded, that meant all the others would come.

He had grown thicker, his step was heavier, but he still had the look of a young wolf. When he got out of the car, he breathed in the air by lifting his muzzle, and he looked all around him before walking along the row of cars. I recognized him right away.

But would he recognize me? So many years gone by. I had aged without realizing it.

I don't know whether it was the intensity of my stare behind the glass wall of the hotel lobby or whether he really saw in me the Old Maid of thirty years ago … He didn't hesitate, his eyes didn't even flicker. He came toward me and gave me a hug.

We spent an eternity between the doors of the entrance, flowing into one another like magnets, until the bustle of the lobby brought us back to reality.

'The Caboose is here. Boy, is he here. He'll be on our heels. He won't leave us be for a minute. But don't worry, no one has told him anything.'

From that point on, confidences would no longer be possible. On the other side of the door awaited the family reunion that we had been dreading for thirty years.

I reluctantly stepped back from my brother's full-grown body, the smell of other countries, the enveloping warmth of his clothes, and together we dove into the rush of emotions.

The conference was a booby trap.

We were all surprised and delighted to be there, but that brief moment of happiness quickly dissolved with the horror of what we saw: we were going to be assembled around Angèle's absence. Our eyes all reflected the same panicked vision of our mother making her entrance at our father's side and, upon seeing her children gathered in the hotel lobby she would count us, as she had in Norco, and discover that Angèle was missing, Angèle, the gentlest, the most likeable, the only one of her children who had a gift for happiness. A sight that would be more than she could handle. A sight that was more vivid to me, as the keeper of the house, than to the others, and I stopped the looks from Cardinals dead in their tracks as they pleaded for me to do something fast to foil the invisible hand that had laid such a cruel trap for us. So there were only a few of us near the front desk when my parents made their entrance.

From then on, it was all just evasion, dodges and equivocations. Our mother was too caught up in her thoughts, wandering the maze of the hotel unaware of our manoeuvres. The Caboose, on the other hand, didn't stop following us, flushing us out wherever we hid. If he sensed our pain, all would be lost. To him, the bottom of the chasm would have the beauty of a Greek tragedy, and he would shout out the nobility of our pain to the world. The Caboose's admiration is incurable.

Tommy was the only one who could save us. She has spent a long time living among the Inuit; she has learned their way of blending into the icy desert. It took me a while before I recognized our insolent, boyish Tommy in this woman of no particular age. She still wears pants and a shirt over a shirt, like back in the day, but she has lost her swagger. With the freshly ironed pants and the shirts, which are actually quite pretty, she has become a strange hybrid, both a warrior and a delicate flower, velvet on a backdrop of ice. With the ice in flames.

She slipped into the crowd. No one noticed her until a booming voice – El Toro's, I think – called out, 'Hey, there's Tommy.' Her dark, velvety gaze fell and, behind it, I saw the rock wall that awaited me if I asked her to save us one more time.

I will never pretend to be Angèle again. Not if they ask me on bended knee, not for money or atonement – never again will I be forced to bear her cross.

Angèle is dead. She died a horrible death, and I won't again wear her smile or the twinkle in her eye, like her standard bearer, with everyone in on it, to keep the family intact.

Angèle is dead. Dead under tons of rock. Crushed to death, mangled, ripped apart, eviscerated, brains spilled out. Dead forevermore. Dead for all eternity. So don't ask me to bring her back.

The Old Maid can hound me all she likes, but her quartermaster's eyes will meet only hard, black stone. Angèle, my Angèle, Angèle of my heart, my sister, my friend. My Angèle is gone, out of harm's way, unseeable, intangible. Her soul fused with mine when she was buried under the rock, and together we withdrew behind a fortress where eyes cannot follow.

Only Noah, my love, my husband, knows where the hidden part of me lives. He has never asked to go there with me. He knows, that's all.

When Noah enters our messy bathroom and sees me smiling in the mirror, he leaves. Softly, on tiptoe.

'Qarinniik uqaqatiqarpit?'

Yes, Noah, I'm talking to my sister. Thank you, Noah. It takes a special man, a special Inuit man, to share his wife with a dead girl's soul. You're more comfortable with the mysteries of life and the hereafter, but how many Inuit women have felt the cut of a savik for no reason?

Noah is my companion at night and in life. He is the most important man in Kangiqsujuaq, the manager of the co-operative.

He studied in the South. He knows the ancient legends, stories and customs of his people, and, at his centre, he has pink, shuddering flesh that explodes in my mouth. The first time, you looked at me, surprised, almost ashamed. It was new to you. Then you didn't resist, you offered yourself to me, and I discovered, incredibly, that I could lose myself in your fleshy thighs, that my entire life could sink into them.

We have been married for over twenty years, and we still reach for each other in the warmth of our bed. We have made three children in that bed, three boys – Tamusi, Joshua and Timarq, three chubby, rambunctious little bears who climbed, ran, hung from anything they could find and left our house in ruins when three female cubs appeared in the wake of their snowmobiles.

Angèle never left me in spite of the boys' boisterousness, in spite of their father's tender, musky flesh, in spite of the emergencies at the health centre. Moments of grace are hard to come by at the health centre, and yet Angèle's smile manages to find its way to me, surreptitiously, softly, while I'm stitching a wound or examining an eardrum. Angèle looks at me and smiles. It's light and velvety. An archangel's feather twirling in my heart. A benevolent thought that protects me. Slowly, I feel a secret joy bubble up and tickle my lips, and I surprise myself by responding, by smiling back at her. The impassive face of the Inuit whose wound I have just sutured can't help but light up in turn. This is why, along the entire Ungava Peninsula, I am known as Qungainnaaq, *The one who smiles.* They come from Koartac, Kangirsuk and Salluit. They have lost their way in the storm or have come to visit family, and they ask for Qungainnaaq.

Angèle's smile is a source of tenderness in my life. When it hasn't appeared inside me in a long time, I settle in before the bathroom mirror and I summon it. I just have to puff out my lips and stretch them a little while pressing them to my teeth for Angèle's smile to be resurrected on my face. It's as easy as that. We were alike, exact duplicates, identical twins. Not a mole, not the tiniest patch of skin distinguished us. We used to kill time by searching our bodies for something to tell us apart. On one of those boring afternoons as summer was drawing to a close, we even tried to count the hairs on our head to see whether we had the same number.

Absolutely identical, and yet so different. The look in your eye, the way you held your head, your gait and, most of all, that heaven-sent smile that fluttered around you like butterflies. Everything about you had the grace and ease of happiness, whereas I was as hard as rock. There was no confusing us. You were Angèle, gentle Angèle, and I was Tommy, a Cardinal, the real deal. When we walked side by side down the streets of Norco, everyone knew who was who.

Happiness. We talked about it a lot, you'll recall, but I wanted no part of it. I had better things to do with my life than to be happy. I had dreams that were so big they were impossible to dream. Happiness was just a burden, a sort of lethargy that was going to sap the spice from my dreams. And life, in one of those cruel reversals of fortune it has a knack for, finds me settled into a sort of happiness in the land of the living, while you were ripped from its promise, dead at seventeen, never having known a loving husband, clean, well-raised children, a house and all the nice clothes that life dangled before you.

'If you can't dream of being happy, I mean, if happiness is something to scorn, what does that leave? Are we supposed to be unhappy? Is the point of life to pursue unhappiness?'

Angèle didn't understand. She didn't want to understand. We had difficult discussions.

I never held it against her. She was under that McDougall woman's spell.

We were five years old when the McDougall woman and her bloated husband set their stinky feet in our house. I will never forget it. They burst the bubble. They made Angèle and me different.

It was Sunday lunch. We were still at the table when the two ghouls – her, tall, dark and nervous, and him, an obese little mouse of a man smiling wide to show off his gold fillings – sat down on the dynamite cases that we pushed up against the wall for them. We were finishing our meal, and they kept staring at Angèle and me.

I didn't understand what they were saying. They were talking to one other, pointing at us and working each other up with empty, limp words, which I didn't understand but which smelled like rotten adult.

We already knew Mr. McDougall. He was part of the gang that paraded through the house: prospectors and money men, schemers and questionable mining-syndicate representatives for whom our father did some prospecting work.

It wasn't like those men to hang around the kitchen, let alone in the company of a woman. Our father received visitors in the basement, where he kept his rocks, his maps and his dreams, and, after long conversations – of which we heard nothing more than a subterranean murmur – they left the house with only a distracted wave for those in it.

The McDougall woman's flesh-eating smile was even more alarming.

She smiled wide at us, baring her big, yellow, witchy teeth, and she wouldn't take her eyes off us. Angèle and I were at the far end of the table, between the Big Kids and that year's baby, so the witch's poisonous gaze escaped no one.

None of the Big Kids had left home at that point. Émilien, the Patriarch, hadn't yet had his dreams of Australia. He was fifteen, which means that there were seventeen of us at the table and that Zorro was the baby. Our mother was at the kitchen counter. She was never far from her pots and pans.

I was only five, but I clearly remember thinking, 'If that witch talks to me or Angèle, I'll scratch a strip off her face.'

We were so connected, so close. It never occurred to me that while I was sharpening my claws, you were letting yourself be quietly devoured by the McDougall woman.

I had a plan for escaping the witch and her runt of a pig. The idea was simple, but I thought it was one of the great military manoeuvres of all time. My idea was to take advantage of the commotion of getting up from the table to slip behind our siblings, who would start fighting over the sofa while arguments in the kitchen over who would do the dishes would distract the two ogres.

The trouble was, with the two ogres there, no one wanted to fight. We got up from the table without incident or injury, and the McDougalls' eyes kept boring into us.

I still tried to escape to the living room, but our father's voice intercepted us: 'Stay here, twins. Mr. and Mrs. McDougall have something to tell you.'

I felt my nails slicing into the palm of my hand. My other hand, the right one, the one that was trying to usher Angèle into the living room, hung there helplessly; Angèle had abandoned it.

She moved toward the two ogres. They were licking their lips, the cannibals. Angèle had flashed her smile, which always sent happiness fluttering.

I was petrified. What were you doing, soul of my soul? Couldn't you tell that they were vampires? That they would suck your blood?

I heard the monsters' words, which our father translated with his limited knowledge of English as they came out of their hideous mouths. Their words offered a glimpse of a tree-lined house, a maple log fire in the living room fireplace, a big beautiful white bedroom for each of us, or if we preferred, an enormous bedroom to share, talking dolls, china dishes, frilly dresses, studies in France or England if we liked. They could give us everything if we agreed to go live with them in Montreal, in a marvellous place called Westmount, which, if we did, would become heaven on earth for them, since they didn't have any children.

The words streamed by, treacherous, deceitful, but I hadn't taken them in yet. I was too absorbed in following Angèle's eyes. She was only a few steps from the monsters, within arms' reach, within claws' reach. She was smiling at them. The angels and archangels fluttered around her. And there was a stubborn gleam in her eye, a light beam fixed on the McDougall woman, following every bob of the horrible child snatcher's head.

She was hypnotized by the McDougall woman's feather. It was the only possible explanation for what happened.

The feather was flitting furiously on the McDougall woman's hat, a horrible hat in faded purple felt, an old-fashioned rich-woman's hat. The feather, bright red and gleaming, whipped the air with a twinkle of light. It was probably fake, plastic, fibreglass at best, but the barbs sparkled like diamonds against the old-fashioned felt. It was the artificial brilliance of the bait that the McDougall woman dispensed in dazzling sprinkles by jiggling and turning round and round like a weather vane unhinged that caught my Angèle's eye and soul in her snare. Because it was toward the poisonous sheen of the feather that she pointed her finger when, throughout the kitchen, an outraged clamour arose.

The Old Maid was the first to voice her indignation: 'What? They want to adopt the Twins?'

And everyone's lips echoed her fury: 'The Twins! They want the Twins!'

It was so unexpected, so grotesque, that nobody could believe it. And yet the McDougalls were there, in our kitchen, sitting on dynamite cases, sickeningly superficial, dripping with desire and holding out their arms to us: 'Do you want to come with us? Do you want to come with us?'

That was when Angèle pointed to the feather and said in the voice of a spoiled child, a voice that we had never heard before: 'I want that.'

The old bag started to coo. 'Oh! Darling! Darling! Darling!'

The McDougall woman was turning into a puddle of joy. She was melting in our kitchen. She was bathing in her own stupidity.

'Oh, darling! Oh, sweetheart!' She hurriedly removed the feather from her hat and held out the faded felt.

I saw – I recorded it in my five-year-old's memory – I saw the pains the McDougall woman took to keep the feather in Angèle's line of sight. She removed the pin, took off the hat and smoothed the hair that tried to cling to it. She cooed and she simpered, but none of her gestures interfered with the shimmering of the feather. She saw to that. The red diamond sparkled with all the fire it had, at Angèle's eye level, when she held out the battered felt to her: 'Here you are, honey. It's yours.'

I was happy, relieved, we all were, to hear Émilien's anger rise up: 'You're not going to let them take the Twins away!'

He was the eldest, our leader, the pride of our family. Geronimo hadn't yet dethroned him, and he was going to show the shrew that it would take more than just flashing the trappings of her wealth to suck us in.

He was standing at one end of the table and addressing our father, who was sitting at the other end, facing the McDougalls, watching the scene with an amused smile. His answer left us with questions we still haven't found answers to.

'The Twins are old enough. It's up to them to decide.'

And that's when – Oh, Angèle, they never forgave you, even me, after all these years, I have a hard time – that's when Angèle moved toward the feather and grabbed the hat. She let the McDougall woman take her in her arms, she sat in her lap and she gave in to the ridiculous, simpering airs of the two scoundrels.

The others didn't believe me. All they could see was the affront, the appearance of what you did. Angèle didn't give herself up for adoption; she was bewitched. She was hypnotized by the damn feather. I know it better than anyone. Angèle and I were of the same flesh. We were of the same essence. I know who she was at that moment, what she felt, what she wanted and what she didn't want. We were a whole that couldn't be divided.

She wanted the feather, just the feather. She didn't want what they offered her afterward, but consented to it, and the others nicknamed her the Foster Child because she accepted the McDougalls' dolls, dresses and finery.

They never forgave her. Geronimo was the most heartless. When he spoke to Angèle, there was a hiss in the air.

I was torn between my allegiance to my family and protecting Angèle. My childhood was over.

What would have become of Angèle, of our poor mother, of all of us, if I hadn't screamed like a banshee?

The McDougalls had Angèle under their spell. They pampered her, whispered obscenities: the big house in Westmount, the trees in front of it, the backyard, the white room and all that happiness dripping with dresses, lace and vanilla ice cream. It was sickening. And while Angèle sullied her soul drooling over plastic twigs, the McDougall woman's eyes flushed me out behind the kitchen ladder where I was holding her dead in my claws, her and her little runt of a husband.

'You want to come with us? You come? Come with your sister?'

The others have told me the whole story, so I know that if the scream hadn't ripped from deep inside me, if my cry had stayed caught in my throat and hadn't broken the spell, my brothers would have advanced in unison and snatched Angèle from their arms. Émilien, Mustang, Yahoo, Fakir, the ones we called the Big Kids, even Tut who was not yet ten, they all told me that they would never have allowed a hick – whether dripping with money or manure, whether from the next town or a big, arrogant city – they never would have allowed a hick to show up at our home and take Angèle.

I roared, I howled, like a lion, like the damned, and I scaled the kitchen ladder.

I can't remember if there was any sense to my howling, if there were words in my outpouring of fury, if I spat out my abuse, my revolt or my pain. I remember only my rage and our mother looking devastated.

My cry broke the spell. Angèle jumped down from the McDougall woman's lap; she ran to the ladder, taking the feathered hat with her, and she came to join me in the laundry room, under the mountain of dirty clothes where I had crouched, and we cried together.

We were only five years old, and yet we knew that the long road that lay before us had suddenly forked. My destiny was clearly mapped: it followed the straight line that would take us all, the proud, peevish Cardinals, to dizzying heights. But what would Angèle do on the wayward road she was taking?

As we were crying in each other's arms, tangled up in all the dirty socks and shirts, we knew that it was our last real moment together, that afterward everything would be different. Angèle didn't go with the McDougalls, but they had taken her soul, and our hearts would no longer beat as one.

The McDougalls went home to their mansion empty-handed. They wanted a matched set, two little identical twins to put in front of their fireplace, and they had been thwarted by my savage cry.

But they kept prowling. The McDougall woman didn't come back, but she sent piles of gifts through her husband. Hats, dresses, petticoats and other trifles of barren women – everything was in lace, ribbon and pairs, in boxes that arrived two or three times a year and that were savagely torn open on the kitchen table so that the short, fat McDougall would know just what we thought of rich people's spew in this house. If it hadn't been for Angèle's wonder-struck eyes, McDougall would have stopped bringing the boxes.

Angèle wore the McDougall's lace and frills innocently, as if she didn't expect that this frivolous display would raise ire and create grudges. I could hear the whole house's disapproval, and every time she wanted to put on one of the rustling dresses I would ask her, 'Why? It's not as if you're going to a ball.' And she would say, gracious and light-hearted, 'It's so pretty. You have to see how it looks in the sun.'

I let her enjoy them, and I did as well. I liked to see the flounces of her dress dancing in the sun. I couldn't help it, even though I knew she heading straight for humiliation.

They didn't hurl abuse or heap criticism on her. Our brothers had finesse when it came to demolition operations. Geronimo was particularly gifted for comments that cut to the quick: 'Where are you going dressed like that? Is it Halloween already in Westmount?' If Angèle continued to swish and pirouette about, if he saw that she was still enjoying the dress, he would propose an expedition: a shed to burn, the brain of a bear to blow up, a raid to punish the hicks. The expedition involved crossing fields and forests, and its sole objective was to make sure the frilly dress saw some action: 'You coming, Foster Child?'

When I see the little girls of Kangiqsujuaq dressed up in flowery dresses under their winter parkas, I can't help but think of Angèle. The little girls of Kangiqsujuaq are plump, sturdy and merry. They wear dresses to celebrate spring, colourful dresses that stand out in the sun. From the window of the health centre, I see them running through puddles, through the garbage the melting snow offers up, through the blocks of ice piled up on the shore of the bay, and I see Angèle, dark skinned like my little Inuit girls, but scrawny, running behind the others through the rubble of Norco. Angèle is wearing her iridescent green tulle dress, her prettiest, the one that best summons the sunshine and joy and that pirouettes, skips and dazzles me with lightness. It's springtime in Norco too. The snow has turned black; it clings to the crumbling remains of the town. Norco has started to look like a battlefield after the fight. And it's a celebration. We're running, Geronimo at the head, off to discover what winter has left for us. But I can't help but see Angèle's pretty dress splashed with mud when Magnum or Big Yellow would run alongside her and jump with both feet in a puddle of dirty water.

It was always like that. They brought her along on raids she didn't want to take part in, and the frilly dress would come back dirty, stained, crusted with clay, soot and sap, full of holes, torn, ruined, fit to join the anonymous heap of clothes in the laundry room.

She had no choice. When Geronimo used that voice to ask her – 'You coming, Foster Child?' – she had to show her allegiance.

It was said in a falsely reverent tone. There was a menacing sarcasm in his way of emphasizing 'Foster Child.' And Angèle, who wanted to prove that she had not gone over to the other side, that she was still ours in spite of her liking for baubles and trim, would agree to ruin her pretty dress in the fields and the forests.

And I no longer knew to whom I owed my loyalty.

Angèle and I were two hearts of the same soul. We lived in symbiosis. We were the Twins, absolutely inseparable, practically Siamese. No one had managed to find anything on either of us that would earn a distinctive nickname, and then a clump of plastic twigs on an old hat stole her soul, and she became the Foster Child.

I didn't wear the dresses the McDougalls sent. I didn't play with their dolls. I said no to skipping ropes, I said no to bubblegum pink, I said no to anything that even remotely resembled the contents of those boxes, and I started playing hockey and baseball and practicing jiu-jitsu, passionately, feverishly, to the point where I earned the position of right wing in hockey and became a force to be reckoned with in jiu-jitsu. I became Tommy.

I was on all the raids, in all the brawls. At age ten, I knocked out Big Boissonneault. At twelve, I defended myself against three kids. I fought with my fists and my feet. But I never scratched or bit like a girl. I defended myself, I attacked, I fought with the intensity of the last man standing.

I fought against the stupidity of the hicks, against the winters that dragged on far too long, against the cruelty of the sun and blackflies in summer, against profound boredom. I fought because I had dreams too big for Norco, because you only get what you take in this life. I fought so that I wouldn't be treated like a girl, so that I wouldn't have to endure Geronimo's sarcasm, so that no one would insinuate anything about the mansion that awaited me in Westmount, and so that no one would ever doubt me. I fought so that you could escape them from time to time, your pretty dress fluttering in the wind, and so that Norco's desolation would light up with the iridescent tulle. I was fighting for you, Angèle.

But of the two of us, you were the more courageous. You and your baubles, you and your archangel's smile, you fought them off better than I could with my tomboyish insolence. In spite of the humiliation, you never gave up your taste for the finer things in life.

Where did that taste come from? I never really understood. From that feather, probably.

'The finer things are just as essential to life as trees and fun. They're as essential as water for fish. A pretty dress is like a flower. It's like the shade of a tree.'

We rejected the finer things, as you well know. 'Fool's gold,' Geronimo called them. We had nothing but disdain for the foreign objects that sneered at our lives from afar. And you wanted a pretty dress to reconcile us with the world?

'That's not what I want. I just want to wear the pretty dresses the McDougalls give me.'

We had these talks often. Angèle would get up on her high horse, and I would try to bring her back to the family fold. The only thing I ever managed to do was torture both of us. She didn't give up the pretty dresses or the mansion in Westmount.

The first time the short, fat McDougall came to get her to take her to the mansion, I thought the world would implode. I wandered around in a daze for two weeks. 'Vacation,' you said before leaving, 'it's just a vacation.'

'A vacation from what? A vacation from who?'

The first time was in the summer of 1957. I remember it well. It was the year the mine closed. The town was in tatters. The price of zinc had collapsed, and with it the hopes of a paycheque among the poor. The town was starting to crack. A few families had left, trailing behind them their houses on makeshift trailers. The others were hesitating between the call of a mine further north and the hope of the price of zinc rising, while, on the mountain, a gang of thugs was dismantling the mine installations. That was just a taste. The serious scramble for the spoils hadn't even started.

'Vacation? When we're going to have the best summer of our whole lives?'

Our mine had been restored to us. We weren't going to cry or pretend. We were the poorest of the poor in this town. Our father wasn't a miner, or a labourer, which would have put him on the mine's payroll and allowed him to lavish gifts on his children. Our father was a prospector, a dreamer through and through. He had discovered the zinc deposit, an enormous one,

2,500 feet by 100 feet, weighing 10 million tons. At the time the newspapers said it was the most important mineral discovery in Canada. Northern Consolidated had drawn up a scam on paper, and he had signed, only too happy to go off and dream somewhere else. And as his children, we would avenge him, would make his royalties worth something, would become kings of the town that he had created – arguments that Angèle couldn't hear.

'I just want to go see their house.'

'A house is just a house: cement, boards, doors, windows. You've seen one house, you've seen them all. It doesn't matter whether it's in Westmount or Norco.'

'They have a doorbell at the front door, a fainting couch in the front hall, velvet drapes, Persian rugs, leather armchairs in the living room and mirrors everywhere in the bathroom.'

' …a fainting couch in the front hall?'

'A couch where you sit lying down.'

'You sit lying down?'

'You see, it's not the same everywhere. I don't know how people sit lying down or why, but I want to find out. I want to see their house. I want to know how people live in other places. I'll come back and I'll tell you all about it, since you won't come. I promise. I swear. I'll come back and tell you everything.'

After the feather, it was the fainting couch. I had nothing to distract her from her fascination with all that glitters somewhere else.

When she climbed into the short, fat McDougall's Oldsmobile, we were on the porch, a silent, solemn family portrait. We were all there. Even our mother. Swept up by the moving crowd, she found herself, a spatula or some other cooking utensil in hand, brutally exposed to the July sun, labouring under the oppressive anger that shimmered in the swelter of emotion. It was clear that we were gathered to withhold our goodbyes from Angèle.

I was there too, immobile, in the front row of the family portrait, clutching my pain to my chest. It's an image that has haunted me all of my life. My first act of treachery.

I would like to be able to erase the image, to strike it from my memory, but to what end, since there were other betrayals, and I can't escape Angèle's eyes looking out from the black Oldsmobile.

Angèle was terrified of the long journey that would take her to the other end of the world, terrified by all the hard, cold faces condemning her for her desertion, terrified by the determination deep down in her heart that was driving her to break loose from us again, terrified, unhappy, desperate, and she looked to me and made a little gesture with her hand. I could barely see her fingers move above the dashboard – you sent me a distress signal, and I let it die at my feet without even looking at it. You weren't asking for much, just for me to detach myself from the wall of resentment and show you with my eyes that I was with you, in solidarity, in spite of the wrath emanating from the porch, and I stayed stony-faced. I let you leave without a farewell. Our first separation. My first betrayal.

The worst part is that you forgave me. As if you already knew what a coward I could be. Yes, the worst part is having seen forgiveness in your eyes. You knew that I couldn't step out of the family portrait, that I had neither the strength nor the courage, nor even the desire, and you smiled a sad, resigned little smile that told me not to worry, that you would bear it all on your own.

The Oldsmobile left, taking you to a place I couldn't even imagine, and I found myself alone, miserably alone, wretchedly alone, with my shame and self-contempt. For two horrible weeks, I fought with the demons in my soul.

During those two weeks, Norco was under the siege of a blazing sun. It was only mid-July, but the air was filled with dry, late-summer dust. Norco was baking. The town was an enclave, a tiny break in the forest, a small, barren island, with no trees or vegetation other than long grass dancing limply between the houses and, subjected to the fiery sky, it had become a huge hotplate that we roamed in every direction, from morning to night, grey from the dust, brown from the sun, black with the rage of conquerors, with me confused in my feelings. I followed the horde, wondering always where you were, what you were doing and whether I should be glad that you had forgiven me.

Geronimo became our leader. It was uncontested, even by Tut or Magnum, who were older but who didn't have Geronimo's insatiable appetite for power. Since the Big Kids had left home, his nerves were stretched taut. At barely twelve years old, it was Geronimo, the restless, destructive little punk, who led us into war. I say war because that's what he called it, so that's what we called it. We were at war. Against the thugs who were dismantling the mining installations, against their slaves, the former miners and the future unemployed of Norco who were helping them pile iron and wood into trucks, against the hicks from neighbouring towns who came to editorialize on the disaster at the hotel, against the wailing, crying and gnashing of teeth, against the earthly powers that had cast an evil spell on our zinc, against the blinding sun that gave us nightmares as we slept. I think we had declared war on the whole planet. And beyond that, on all the forces of the universe that kept us there, in that devastated humanity, fiercely attached to our poverty, and convinced that the pure, hard essence of the diamond that was within each one of us would rise from our self-denial.

I was never so fiercely a Cardinal as during those two weeks. I was on all the commando raids. A raid on the mountain? I was the first to volunteer. I would spy on the thugs, steal their tools and gas, slash their tires and, the ultimate pleasure, throw a match in a shed, running to take shelter with the others and watch, if luck was on our side, the wood burning, the shed in flames, the machinery, all of it going up in thick smoke so it couldn't be shipped off for use at another mine. As for the hicks, both our own and those of neighbouring towns who came to lament their fate at the Hôtel Impérial or the Hôtel Royal, they went home with a dead fish or cat in their car, if the car started of course, if we hadn't shoved a potato up the exhaust pipe. And then there were all the fires breaking out in the dry grass.

I threw myself headlong into the war. There were so many knots tangled up in my pain: shame, self-contempt and the offence, mine and yours, that I took it upon myself to atone for. Was it the porch of shame I was running away from? I don't know whether my fury in combat was meant to help me forget that you weren't there, that you had deserted, or whether it was my own defection that I wanted to be pardoned for, my secret love of your dresses in the sun, the endless tenderness that I still had for you in spite of my siblings' stubborn anger.

Only during the long nights did I find a bit of relief. I tried to imagine you at the McDougalls', but I had never seen a fainting couch, or even a front hall or a doorbell. I couldn't think straight. I couldn't imagine you in the land of the rich, and the night unfolded, long, black and sleepless, until our mother came to the bedroom where I was sleeping. She would look at me for a long time. I would feel her eyes on my closed eyelids, and after a moment, she would bend over me, softly, and brush my cheek with her weary hand: 'Go on, sleep. Don't worry. She'll come back.' I would finally sleep, reassured by the image of the black Oldsmobile bringing you home.

The town was still smoking when you came home. We no longer settled for throwing matches at random. Now we had a weapon for lighting fires from a distance, placing them right where we wanted – a distinct improvement since, having become public enemy number one, we now had a commando unit of little brats on our tail.

The bow and cattail. Magnum's invention, I believe, and our greatest feat of arms. A supple branch of birch stretched on fishing line, and a cattail soaked in oil or gas. September cattails made the best torches. Thick and cottony, they soaked up the gas, and flames roared at the first strike of the match. But in that terrible summer of drought, July cattails were just as thirsty, and all it took was for one of our torches to brush the tip of a tuft of grass for the fire to spread into an inferno.

Fire set off in every direction and in just about every location that summer. Garbage-can fires, brush fires, grass fires: they spread virtually everywhere, along ditches, in vacant lots, near houses. They scorched a litter of kittens and burned Vaillancourt's stockpile of old tires, licked the brick of the Potvins' house and nibbled the edge of the forest several times. The fires even had the nerve to surround the fire station. But they were mainly on the mountain, around the mining camp. In fact, we were aiming for the dynamite store.

When people came running from every direction to put out the fire, we came running too with our shovels and rakes, and we fought the flames alongside our fine, brave fellow citizens, who, eyes red with rage and smoke, shouted at us, 'Get out of here! Bloody hoodlums!' They raged in their impotence. They couldn't touch us. There were too many of us. Our parents had left us to our own devices, and we were growing like weeds.

By the end of the summer, many families had left Norco. Tired of hoping against hope, exhausted, worn out, broken by the sun and the war we were waging, the families left, with or without their houses, their beaters filled to bursting with their brood, boxes and piles of junk. And before leaving town, they would make a detour past our house, their old cars hiccupping under the load, and in a din of beeping, clanking and shouting, the father, the mother and the children, their faces wild with rage, their fists raised, their eyes bulging, would insult us, as they had never dared: 'Stay here and rot in hell, you savages! Wallow in your own shit, you retards!' We had won.

When the short, fat McDougall's Oldsmobile appeared at the bend in our road, we were just beginning to experiment with the bow and cattail. But we had a fire going nonetheless, and El Toro was the one who spotted the glint of the Oldsmobile's metal through the smoke: 'Angèle's here! Look, Angèle's here!'

'You mean Miss McDougall.'

Geronimo's grudge hadn't ebbed. Not even then, with you coming back.

So, rather than running home at full tilt, as we wanted to do, we reminded each other that you had deserted us and forced ourselves to walk at a normal pace.

You looked like a princess. You were like a breath of fresh air, a spring flower in the midst of the acrid smell of scorched fields. The dress, all white and weightless shimmer, the shoes, the gloves, the hat, right down to the delicate little necklace of satiny beads, everything had the alabaster beauty of a creature from heaven. You were enchanting.

Were you even aware of the image you projected? You, so white in front of the black Oldsmobile, and us, tousled and ragged, evil gnomes emerging from scorched earth. Had you forgotten the wrath? Our show of strength on the porch?

I really believe that those two weeks of pampering with the rich folks had made you lose all notion of survival in the family. You were beaming, trusting in the beauty of your finery, and you weren't on guard.

The first strike came from Big Yellow.

'Good afternoon, Miss McDougall.'

Nefertiti or Wapiti or another of the Weewuns, I don't remember which, repeated in their childhood innocence: 'Goonoon, MiGall.'

Geronimo was the most cutting. Our young chief had to demonstrate the knife-edged cruelty of his intelligence to stay leader of the pack.

'So, was two weeks licking gold doorknobs enough?'

And by placing his soot-blackened hands on the collar of the dress, he gave the signal for the massacre.

They approached, one after the other, pawing the fancy fabric, lifting the layers of crinoline, their sticky hands admiring the beads, ribbons and lace, and when there was no white left, when there was nothing more to set her apart, they put a shovel in her hands, and Angèle, the poor mortified thing in her blackened dress, followed them toward a grass fire that they offered by way of welcome.

Once again, I was left to savour the bitter disillusion of my cowardice. I was the one who had said the thing about the gold doorknobs to Geronimo a few days before.

He had wanted to humiliate me. We were in the heat of the action, quite literally. We had just let a torch fly in the direction of the dynamite store. There was Bibi, Big Yellow, Tintin, Matma – there were seven or eight of us in all, lying in wait behind a rubble chute, Geronimo and me on the front lines of the battle, and he said to me, turning toward the others so that his innuendo-laden smile escaped no one:

'Shouldn't you be at your mansion?'

In that moment, all I could think of was defending my honour, and I answered:

'Yeah, right! Spending two weeks licking gold doorknobs is not for me, no thank you!'

He was feeling insecure in his position as leader. I was too keen on fighting, and he wanted to crush me before I threatened his fragile authority. That's how I see it now, with almost forty years' hindsight, but at the time, we were living on a knife edge, me more than the others because of my dual allegiance, and the only thing I could think then was *every man for himself*, forgetting the part of me that should have protected you.

After having disowned you, how could I be close with you again?

You always forgave me, for both my minor flaws and my major cowardice, the things that I confessed to and things that you couldn't even suspect, and I continued to live my double life, protected by my boyish ways and your forgiveness, without realizing that one day I would have to choose.

There were other humiliations, other betrayals. The McDougall woman's short, fat husband came back to take you away every summer in mid-July. The departures and the home-comings were always just as painful, but I no longer took your absence quite so hard, because now I could imagine you at the McDougalls' house.

I knew the colour of the walls, the living room drapes, the kitchen linoleum and the quilt on your bed. I knew what a fainting couch was, a cheval glass, venetian blinds, white marble, jasper marble, English porcelain, pedestal ashtrays, step-on garbage cans – you explained it all to me, told me everything. I could imagine you in every room in the house.

There were seventeen rooms, if you counted the maid's quarters under the eaves, where sometimes you went to rest – 'luxury can get exhausting' – but I saw you most often in the big white bedroom, surrounded by curtains that billowed gently, with smiling images, elegant furniture and toys, each one stranger than the last, which you taught me about. Round, colourful dolls that disappeared one inside the other, 'nesting dolls'; long slender dolls that you dressed and undressed, 'Barbies'; dolls that talked, walked and peed, and everything needed to bring them to life: the carriage, the cradle, the little chrome table, the dishes and even a three-storey house, practically a miniature replica of the McDougalls' house, which you redecorated every day, crouching between the two open halves, singing 'Jack and Jill went up the hill' to yourself.

'"Jack and Jill"? How did you know I would sing "Jack and Jill"?'

'Because I heard you singing it.'

'How can you have heard me when you weren't there?'

I heard you, I saw you, I was there, with you, in that house that smelled like almond pastry and wilted roses. I just had to unlock the surface of my mind, and I was transported to Westmount, Lexington Avenue, to a house that had been described to me in minute detail, which I could inhabit with every fibre of my being. It was a trick that took some time to perfect and that consoled me during Angèle's absences all those years she spent becoming part of the middle class at the McDougalls', and, later, at boarding school.

At first, Angèle didn't believe me. 'That's impossible. You're pulling my leg.' She asked for details, specifics. She tried to catch me out on little things, a ring she had lost or the maid who had given her a gift. She would try to trip me up ('the dog almost bit me, here, under my right eye'), offer counterfeit images ('Mr. McDougall took Brandy to the SPCA'), but I knew what I had seen. 'Her name is Candy, not Brandy. And she didn't even touch you. She barely growled when you tried to take her dish away, and it was the maid who took her to the SPCA.'

She had no choice but to believe me. I was there, with her, at the McDougalls', leaving an empty shell in Norco, which my mother bent over during her nightly rounds. Our poor mother must have been puzzled by the little girl with eyes wide open in the dark. I often had to hurry back to reassure her and give her the sleepy smile she wanted as she shook me gently: 'Carmelle, wake up. You've gone too far into your dream.'

I was never so happy as in those moments when Angèle appeared to me at the outposts of my being. I stretched my mind as far as it would go, burrowing into the pain until there was nothing left of me, until the absolute emptiness became vertigo, and that's when Angèle, lighthearted and smiling, appeared on the flat surface of my awareness and beckoned me to follow her.

I always saw her smiling. At the McDougalls', in the downy comfort of money, and, later, at the Sisters of the Assumption, the Pensionnat Sainte-Marie, where the money paid for a classical education, and she was deliriously happy.

It was different at the boarding school. There were all those black veils, long corridors, the uniformity of life, and Angèle's smile would cloud over a little. In spite of the more discreet smile, I could see that she was happy in the austere setting, which was still much more pleasant than home.

There were moments when I was afraid that she wouldn't want to come back to us. The homecomings were so difficult and life at boarding school was so gentle for someone whose heart tended toward the finer things: *Rosa, rosa, rosae*, Romulus and Remus, Scipio Africanus, Zeus and Jupiter, classical culture, high culture, culture that unlocks the doors of respect and consideration. The keys to the world were handed to her with all the honours due to the first in the class. Why would she agree to leave that peaceful world for the den of the deranged, who started quarrelling over the scraps of her soul as soon as she set foot in the house?

'Family is an encounter with the deepest parts of your soul.'

When she would return each month from boarding school, after the snub of the homecoming, after they had unleashed enough wrath on the convent uniform, Angèle and I would find a quiet corner where we could pick up the previous month's conversation. These moments alone were our only anchor, and it was during these secret conversations that I discovered her deep faith in happiness and, above all, her attachment to the family.

'I'm a Cardinal and always will be, no matter what they do, or what I do.'

Our time alone was constantly under threat from the malicious pleasure the others took in hunting us down. Geronimo couldn't indulge in such childishness anymore – he was sixteen, seventeen, eighteen at the time. But his sneering smile watched over the younger ones, the ones he sent out to track us, normally El Toro, Zorro, Pester, sometimes one of the Weewuns too. He told them, 'Your sister Angèle should recite something in Latin,' or 'It's been a long time since she told us about good ol' Caesar's military campaigns,' and the little brothers would set off on our heels. They would find us in a corner of the basement, in the laundry room hiding behind a mountain of clothes, sometimes even under a bed with all the dust bunnies, and they would bring us back to the living room, in front of the three-seater sofa, where Geronimo waited for us, the great lord and master of the game. 'So, how are things with the Gauls? Last month, if I remember correctly, Vercingetorix was giving Caesar a pretty rough time.' And Angèle, in front of the assembled family, had to spout off her bits of Latin culture. She was being shamed. It was the whole point of the game.

In spite of the confusion and disorder of the rooms, the house offered no safe haven. They would always find us. The same for the town. Since the mine had closed, and particularly since the start of our bombardment, the town had become deserted. Only a dozen inhabited houses remained; the others had been ripped from their squares of concrete or left to our tender care, so there was no point in seeking refuge among the ruins. Norco had become Cardinal territory. There was not a carcass or a ruin of a house that wasn't familiar, down to the tiniest creaks and moans.

In the end it was at the church, under Father Prudhomme's protection, that Angèle and I had these delicate, difficult conversations.

Father Prudhomme left us to the devotions of our confidences, in front of the side altar dedicated to the Virgin Mary, and if a pack of little brothers appeared at the end of the nave or in a half-open door, all he had to do was draw himself up to his full stature and invoke his power as a holy man of the woods, and they would run off without a peep. He was the only person in Norco who could do that.

The faded little altar to the Virgin is where I most like to picture Angèle. It is bare, poorly decorated, but with nice light. A recess for contemplation in the vast emptiness of the church. The air is fresh, and you can hear the wind blow between the windows. And beside me, on the polished wooden bench, Angèle is there in her convent uniform, Angèle telling me about the dreams she dreamed at boarding school. Angèle who is certain that a big, beautiful life awaits her, Angèle who talks, thinks, wonders and keeps smiling and trying to convince me that there is nothing wrong with wanting to be happy.

I can see us. I can hear us as clearly and surely as when you went sashaying about at the McDougalls' or when you were being clever at the Sisters of the Assumption, and, when, left on my own, I followed you so I wouldn't get lost. You never felt my presence? You never felt that I was there, beside you, among the students with starched collars reciting Lamartine and Rimbaud? I still ask, like I did so many times, 'You didn't sense my presence?'

You looked at the flames of the votive candles burning in front of the statue of Mary, and you said no, you were sorry, and the smell of burnt wax became unbearable. I haven't set foot in a church since Norco.

You told me that at the convent you had discovered pure beauty, and that my voice didn't reach you because there was always music playing in your head. The music of Mauriac, Giraudoux, De Montherlant, all the great bards of the French language, and Gide above all, André Gide and *The Fruits of the Earth*, from which you quoted entire passages, passages that heightened the pleasure of life, your desire for it, and that left me speechless. Do you remember? You told me not to worry, that the rich girls I saw you laughing with and talking to at the convent weren't your friends, that your soul was here, with me, with all of us, your brothers and sisters, in spite of your longing for another life.

We were fifteen, sixteen. We were swept up in dreams that were urging us to leave adolescence behind. We didn't doubt that one day we would achieve our personal glory, you reigning over exquisite pleasures, somewhere on cloud nine, and me ... 'And what exactly will you reign over? Over the gold you despise? Over the love you'll deny?' You could be so harsh.

We could have stayed there, having the searching conversations of teenagers. We could have lasted a long time against the diabolical cycle of indignities, humiliations and betrayals that we ended up getting used to, and one day we would have left Norco, intact, with our cache of hopes. We would have gotten what we wanted out of life. Instead I am haunted by a vision of you crushed under tons of rock, broken, destroyed, gone forever.

And now I have to save the day? I have to slip into your grace and your smile, and take your likeness for a walk down the hallways of the Quatre-Temps, the image of you alive, so that they can keep up appearances?

No, I won't pretend anymore. Only at home, in Kangiqsujuaq, in our cracked bathroom mirror, will I bring you back to life. I do it for me, just for me, to feel the pleasure and the pain. I settle in at the mirror. I stare into it hard, my lips stretch, my eyes start to shine, and I watch you appear, as you were, a little girl with the dancing eyes, an excited teenager, a dreamer, and I see you as you would be now, at forty-seven, the companion and friend with whom I would share the pleasures of my marriage, large and small, my anxiety as a mother about the future of my three mixed-race boys, and my solitude. I would entrust you with my solitude, my profound solitude. Angèle, wherever you are, can't you feel my presence?

Sometimes the metamorphosis happens without my meaning it to. During long solitary walks by the bay, to the landing strip and beyond, almost to the edge of the hinterland. Hours and hours of fresh air, walking at a steady pace, with a limitless horizon, and, little by little, in the middle of my humdrum thoughts, I feel my step lighten, my muscles becoming graceful and supple. That's when I know that the miracle will happen inside me, that my entire being will reach toward you, that I will take on your eyes, your smile, the swing of your arms and your legs. And soon, in the icy solitude of Nunavik, it isn't the nurse from the Kangiqsujuaq clinic that the rock ptarmigan is watching go by, but Angèle Cardinal, little Angèle who walks with a lighter step to meet her happiness.

Like when we were in Norco and the desire suddenly came over me to be you, do you remember? I transformed before your eyes in an instant. You laughed and asked me, 'Do I really look like a lost doll?' I liked hearing you laugh.

I was wearing your sky-blue dress the first time I felt my body slip into yours. You never knew it. I never told you. I didn't want you to know that I was drawn to all those sparkling, shimmering dresses I tried to save you from. In spite of my bravado, inside me there was a little girl who didn't dare admit that she was attracted to the fickle charms of femininity. I knew what it had cost you.

But one day, I found myself alone with one of your dresses and I couldn't resist. It was laid out on the bed, puffed up with flounces and lace, sparkling with light, the picture of pride. A blue organdy dress with little white flower accents embroidered in a crisscross pattern, and it sparkled in a sunbeam under the only window in the bedroom. It made my head spin.

I was alone in the bedroom, alone on the whole second floor, or at least that's what I thought, and I put on the dress without thinking.

Once the cotton muslin touched my legs, I wanted to dance and twirl, like a fairy-tale princess, the picture of happiness – like you did every time you put on a dress for the first time. It was pure pleasure. I was light, graceful, delicate, a china doll on a high wire, and life opened its arms to me. Everything around me was goodness and smiles. I was dancing on a cloud. And I was swept up in a gentle whirlpool until I felt El Toro's sharp, mocking eyes, and I realized that the euphoria of the dress had swept me out of the bedroom, into what we called the study, and that I had been exposed.

El Toro didn't waste a second. He was convinced he was looking at Angèle. He was excited to have you in his power, alone, without the entire pack behind him while he cut his teeth on you. You were older than him, but so soft and tender, the ideal prey for a young wolf looking for an easy kill.

He puffed himself up with all the toughness he could find, and he said something nasty, the first thing that came to mind.

'Well, if it isn't McDougall. I'm surprised your head can get through the door.'

I turned back into Tommy.

He was about to go on, when he realized something was wrong. I felt his eyes change; he had figured it out. He wanted to come closer to get a good look at what he could hardly believe, but I was faster.

'You, if you ever …'

My fist was cocked, and my face was flushed. I would have beaten the crap out of him, kicking and punching, if necessary,

I was so terrified by the idea that he was going to tell the others what he had seen.

Luckily, he retreated into a corner, and I didn't have to fight him. I went back to the bedroom, determined to deny it if it got out, and, more importantly, determined never to give in to the temptation of your dresses again.

The desire didn't go away, though. The desire for silky fabric on my skin, the puff of the crinoline on my legs, the desire to walk with small winged steps, to feel the ground drop from under me, to fly, lifted by the weightlessness of the dress, and the desire to shimmer in the sun. These mad ideas stayed with me, and I often found myself walking like a ballerina, arms outstretched as if held aloft by layers of crinoline and flounces, my body poised to take flight. I think I would have lifted off if I had been discovered, in pants and two layers of shirts, in a pantomime that anyone could stumble on at any moment.

I grew cautious and learned to transform at will, discreetly, without risk, just to make you laugh. It was our little secret.

Now I do it only in my white woman's solitude, a Qallunaaq lost in the North.

On the runway, just before the plane took off, Noah asked me: 'Qarinniik aullaqatiqalarpik?'

I answered no, I wasn't bringing my sister with me. But words hide nothing between us; we are connected by something much more important than lovers' chitchat, and he instinctively recognized your presence: 'Iiq! Takunnataugnnuk.'

So I turned off that look in my eye so you wouldn't be seen. When I walked into the Quatre-Temps, no one recognized Tommy or Angèle in the solemn, hunched woman I manoeuvred slowly toward the front desk. It took El Toro and his booming voice announcing my arrival from the other end of the lobby for them to turn when I passed.

I see or talk to El Toro every three or four years, when he comes to do a report on the North or phones me for information or an introduction to a Makivik official. I am his source for all things Inuit and the Great North. But I hadn't seen the others – who were looking at me as if I had emerged from the depths of their consciousness – since I left Norco.

The Old Maid can follow me with that overbearing look of hers, the Caboose can circle me like a starved animal and the others can signal their distress, but it's too late for miracles. It's too late, do you hear me? Too late for regrets, too late for pain. Angèle is dead. The only place she will come back to life is inside me, and I won't give her back to you. I won't conjure her with my eyes, with my smile, to create the illusion of a big happy family.

The days are gone when I would sacrifice myself for the good of the family. The days are gone when they could ask me to convince Bibi, poor Bibi, who was in love with a Boissonneault and who watched her stomach swelling, to get it taken care of by a backstreet abortionist that the Big Kids had dug up in Montreal. I never felt right about the speech I gave her about the wrong mix of chromosomes. Poor Bibi, the poor girl, alone and isolated in a family of boys, the poor girl to whom I never paid more than passing attention.

The days are gone when they could ask me for whatever they wanted, provided they left me alone.

I am Carmelle Sakiagaq now, wife of Noah, mother of Tamusi, Joshua and Timarq, and you can plead with me with your eyes, but nothing will force me to bring Angèle to life in the hallways of the Quatre-Temps.

There are moments that are worth a lifetime. I knew that I would find what I was looking for in the first glance they exchanged. As soon as I saw Tommy, I positioned myself to watch her advance through the crowded lobby until she was in the Old Maid's line of sight and, in the loudest voice I could, I announced, 'Tommy's here!' That's when, in the searing intensity of the looks exchanged, I found the missing piece of my puzzle. But no one guessed what El Toro – Lucien by birth – was hatching.

I've been probing a bottomless pit for so long – I wonder if I can truly be at the end of my quest.

First I had to figure out that Angèle died in the accident at the mine. Like the others, I had seen her get into Émilien's car after the accident. Like the others, I had seen her, looking well, almost smiling, in the back seat of the car, and then I never saw her again.

Was I already a journalist at heart or did I become one by dint of stalking the silences and the looks exchanged whenever Angèle's ghost haunted a conversation?

I had no reason to doubt Angèle's leaving or the lingering image of her. It was entirely plausible that she had gone to study in Montreal. She liked school, and she was drawn to polite society. And anyway, things were falling apart at home.

It was what was said afterward and passed along sibling to sibling, with insistence and conviction, that planted the seeds of doubt in my mind. Regular information that was both contradictory and peremptory and that told a story of an incredibly successful life, a life worthy of any of our dreams, and one that kept her away, always farther away, but alive. She had studied history, philosophy, sociology and who knows what else at Université de Montréal, McGill or Sir George Williams, it didn't matter. The important thing was that the school be prestigious. Then she worked at Radio-Canada, the United Nations, UNESCO, on diplomatic missions and at embassies. She travelled a lot, in Europe, Asia and Africa. We lost track of her somewhere, but I no longer believed all the globe-trotting. I knew she was dead.

It took years of doubts and feeling my way in the dark to become sure of it.

Every time I interviewed a prominent bureaucrat at the United Nations or UNESCO, someone who could have run into Angèle in the course of her career, near the end I would make sure to turn the interview to personal matters and ask my question. Obviously, my subjects didn't know Angèle. The answer never surprised me. I was just trying to confirm what I had long guessed.

I knew she was dead, all the evidence pointed to it, but I needed some doubt. I needed to think that she had escaped the accident, and escaped our awareness.

In fact, in all those years, I never stopped chasing the image of Émilien's old Studebaker taking Angèle far away. The image is vivid, even though it's fake. It looks like the image of Angèle leaving for the McDougalls, which infuriated us. Angèle wouldn't be coming back this time wearing one of her ridiculous dresses. She had taken herself out of the image. She had made her peace with herself and left us to our fate.

In that final image where I see her almost smile, her head held high, she doesn't even look at us. She is sitting in the back seat, her things gathered around her in brown paper bags, and she is waiting for Émilien to finish his preparations. He walks around the car, checks each tire with a kick, tests the shocks by putting all his weight on the hood, then lifts it, checks the oil.

He has owned a Ford and a Rambler, but the Studebaker is his pride and joy.

Geronimo is in the front seat. He is leaving forever too. The only time we will ever see him again is on TV, being interviewed about the wars he has chased after, scalpel in hand, offering cold comment.

He is uneasy. He is chain-smoking, tapping on the car door, untying and retying his tie. I have never seen him so nervous.

Our leader was leaving, our mentor, the brains of the operation. There had been moments of revolt against the firm hand of his authority, but we never prevented his rise. His hazing, his remarks that humiliated us to the quick, his predator's eye, which stung more than the lash of a whip, and the beatings that were inflicted on us with the devastating precision of lightning: we knew all of that was a way of steeling us for the battle we would have to wage against life. Even Angèle understood that.

He had to leave, and fast, because we would be called to account. All of us watching the preparations for departure knew that we would be held responsible for the accident. I was thirteen at the time, and I was keenly aware of the danger looming. They would come, and we would have to play it pretty cool to avoid having the finger pointed at us. If it wasn't the police, it would be the people from New Northern Consolidated or the Norco hicks.

The worst were the hicks, the few little shits who had resisted and who might think their hour of glory had come, thanks to the disaster. But their last hope went up in smoke in the accident. They were pathetic. They had refused to leave their shacks and their lives of misery when everyone was abandoning Norco. In spite of the poverty, in spite of the hope growing dimmer with the years, they had hung on to the promise of the land of Cain, waiting for a miracle to give them back their mine and hand out riches by the fistful.

There were only nine inhabited enclaves left in the land of Cain. The Boissonneaults, the Laroses, the Morins, the Desrosiers. I could name them all – first name, last name, age, eye colour. Life in Norco was a constant battle between the Cardinals and all the others.

They would forgive us nothing. Our games, our bravado, our demented challenges, the grass fires we brought to their door, the bears we tormented to the point of madness that then besieged the town, muzzles torn by dynamite caps, and all the half-rotted cat carcasses that we carried in a procession through the potholed streets, their futile anger when they recognized their cat impaled on one of our spikes. The humiliation, the shame, the fear – they would not forgive us for having rubbed their noses in their own stupidity. But most of all, they would not forgive us for dashing their dreams.

Maybe they had settled into their poverty. Maybe they were using the dream of renewed prosperity to warm the bones of their misery. Maybe their dream was an illusion kept alive with no real hope. But it was all they had left of their dignity and they were going to want revenge.

The accident had happened just before Émilien, Geronimo and Angèle took their places in the counterfeit tableau. The tremor, more than the noise, was what had raised the alarm. Nothing actually moved, but we all felt it in our bodies when the earth lurched. There were three explosions – on that, we could all agree. The first, muffled and strong, followed by the second, which was booming, and finally, the third, which crescendoed into a terrible roar.

Even before the third explosion, we were all outside and running toward the mountain, where – we knew, we hoped with all our might – we would find the mine, our mine, out of commission, to anyone and everyone for centuries to come.

The hicks, rushing in a herd to the site of the disaster, joined us to watch the earth sink into the earth, the rock being sucked into the rock. The explosion had hit the heart of the mine, opening a pit that swallowed up huge masses of rock. We saw the last swallows of the subterranean depths. It threw up a thick cloud of dust and a strong, distinct odour that left no doubt as to the source of the disaster: the smell of dynamite.

They were too hick to openly accuse us. They had arrived on the mountain at top speed and joined our circle around the crater left by the explosion, but as the smell of dynamite became evident, they couldn't bear to be near us, and they withdrew. One by one, moving sluggishly, they left our ranks and gathered in a ball of hatred near the mine office. They were all there: men, women and children. And they kept repeating Geronimo's name: 'Where's Geronimo? Geronimo's not here? Has anyone seen Geronimo?'

Where was Geronimo? Behind us, concealed by the dust or hiding out in a building, watching the scene from the beginning, rushing to get rid of the traces of the explosion on his clothes? We never knew whether he had just arrived or had been there all along.

He emerged from the ranks and turned to face them. On top of his game. His voice didn't waver. He didn't flinch.

'What do you want?'

In the teeming mass, someone grumbled, 'Oh, come on. You know perfectly well. You'll pay for this.' The accusation was there, in their eyes, in the muted bleating of their voices, in the fists they wanted to use on us and that were held tight against their thighs. They couldn't confront us openly.

A short time later, Geronimo sat in Émilien's Studebaker, and no one bothered to check whether, in the back seat, Angèle was indeed Angèle.

It was a summer's day, one of those days that burn you up head to toe and leave you without a single drop of sweat to dry in the sun. Summer in Norco was like the Sahara until August. We lived in a vortex of dry steam under a sky shimmering cruelly until, out of pity, the clouds would burst and send torrential rain pounding down on us for weeks.

The night before, we had celebrated Pester's birthday. He had turned eleven, and we went to celebrate the event at the quarry, as was the family tradition. It was a nice enough explosion, though a bit anemic for my tastes. I like a blast with something to it, one that lifts itself off the ground like a furious beast and spits destruction in every direction. Pester's, unfortunately, suffocated before it was born. The sand, which had been heated white hot for weeks, was little more than dust. The dynamite blast coaxed nothing more than a big powdery fart out of it, which evaporated in a diffuse circle. It was a letdown.

The Big Kids were there for the occasion. They had come from Montreal, Quebec City and even Toronto, with the shine of big-city glory on them. No one had been abroad yet. Émilien was just starting to dream of Australia; he had brought with him a pamphlet full of blue skies, sheep-speckled grasslands and broad Aboriginal smiles. The pamphlet was a challenge to us. It represented the freedom to roam the continents – it was the world in the palm of our hands. These samples of life were part of what made the Big Kids wise.

The house was full to bursting. We didn't have enough beds, chairs or time. There weren't enough hours for the spectacle that was our family.

The discussions were never-ending. The Big Kids brought news of the big city. We told them about our latest skirmishes, and together we circled the globe, with mandatory stops at anything that raised our indignation and provided an opportunity to rail against the stupidity of people, which I loved to do. I think these conversations were what led me to journalism.

In the kitchen, in the living room, on the porch and even upstairs, it was a rapid fire of voices talking over one another, all fuelled by the same lust for life. We wanted to rebuild the world on the foundations of an ideal that was ours alone. A world striving toward the ultimate achievement, a work of uncompromising truth. 'Life is not for the faint hearted,' Geronimo would say.

I was still too young to join in, but I agreed with everything that was said, and I didn't want to miss a thing. I went from the living room to the kitchen, from the kitchen to the study. I went up and down the kitchen ladder, and I climbed the outdoor stairs. I was always on the move, looking for the most important conversation of the moment.

Most often I would find myself in the living room, where Geronimo, Big Yellow and Fakir were, our most fervent speechifiers, and where the three-seater sofa was, which, although sagging and gaping in a number of spots, was still the best seat in the house. There were no sofa battles; a truce took hold, but for laughs, for the Big Kids, who had felt an amused nostalgia for it, each of us said *Smyplace*, distinctly and consciously, even if all we had to give up was a corner of dusty floor.

Our father came into the living room a few times. He never stayed long. All of that youth intimidated him, I think, and he went back to his fog of dreams in the basement.

Most of all I remember our mother, in her nightgown, barefoot as usual, with her smile of the Madonna. She was spent from her efforts with her pots and pans, having cooked one of her fabulous meals, and she was nodding off in a chair in the corner of living room. Her nightly rounds had long been a thing of the past.

That family gathering was our last. The next day was the accident at the mine. Geronimo and Émilien left, taking the counterfeit image of Angèle with them.

When there is no coffin, no funeral, no burial, it is hard to reconcile yourself with the unacceptable. Even once it became inescapable, I rejected the idea of Angèle's death, and I clung to the doubt created by the half-smiling image in the Studebaker.

It took the smallest of things for the comfort of doubt to disappear forever. All it took was the beginnings of a smile. Angèle's smile on Tommy's lips.

It was years after that July afternoon. Only a few of us still saw each other. The Cardinals had started to disband. Émilien was in Australia, Fakir was in Vancouver, Big Yellow was somewhere in Latin America, not to mention Geronimo, Pester, Matma and Tut, from whom there had long been no word. No one was surprised when one of us disappeared.

I had started a career as a journalist, which I was suitably impressed by. I worked at *La Presse*, a fine place for the ambitious, and I fired on anything that moved. I was young, hungry for success and very lonely.

And it was by chance during a long solitary walk that I discovered another solitude, a woman who was looking for the moon in the towering glass of the buildings. Tommy, my sister.

She was walking slowly in front of me. The night was cold, freezing really – it was January, the cruellest winter month – and this woman was wandering the streets of Montreal, carefree and nonchalant as a bather on the beach.

Without realizing it, I started to keep pace with her, and it was only when we reached Marie-Anne Street that she turned toward me – 'Just what is it you want from me?' she said – and I realized that I was following her.

It took me a moment to recognize her. She had deep wrinkles around her mouth, her face had grown fuller, and, most significantly, there was a disquietingly powerful immobility inside her. But Tommy, the moon hunter, recognized me immediately: 'El Toro ... ! Is that you? What on earth do you want?'

To talk, that's all I wanted. To talk about her, about me, to talk about everything and nothing at all, to talk to pick up the thread of our lives. We hadn't seen each other since we had both left Norco.

We went into a nearby bar, and we spent what was left of the night talking. She listened carefully, both smiling and serious, and kept the conversation focused on me: me and my job, me and my love life, me and everything I fed with my hope and bitterness. She clearly didn't want to talk about herself, either in the present or the past.

I was vaguely aware that she had become a nurse in the North and that she had married an Eskimo. 'An Inuit,' she specified, when I managed to raise the topic. '*Eskimo* means *eater of raw meat*, a name the White Man gave us that everyone in the North rejects. *Inuit*, in Inuktitut, means *real man*, and that's the right word for us.'

Us? I couldn't help but notice the *us*, which made me feel queasy, but she had taken refuge behind her steady stare and I didn't pursue it.

I did manage to find out that she was on a mission, escorting a young Inuit man to the hospital, Hôtel-Dieu, I think – 'acute peritonitis,' she explained – and that she was having a hard time finding the peace of what she called her moon days.

'I don't eat seal meat, but I eat mattaq and panirtitaq. I use an ulu to cut meat, and I have three boys with Inuit features who won't come with me when I come down South. So when I go for a walk in your moonless night, I can't help but think how much I have become an Inuit. But at home, in Kanjirsujuaq, I'm a Qallunaaq, a white woman.'

All the *q*'s and *g*'s that she formed at the back of her throat made me feel queasy again. I had had more than one whisky.

And Angèle, have you forgotten her? Have you forgotten Angèle while you've been stuffing mattaq and panirmachintaq in your face? Have you thrown your whole past overboard to become the docile wife of an Inuit man?

I wanted to shake her, force her to open up another side of her life to me. And what about us, Tommy, have you forgotten us? Have you forgotten what keeps us in Norco? A whole battalion of questions that I had to hold back, because I knew that the fiery eyes veiled in velvet would stop me from going any further than what we had tacitly agreed upon from the start.

And it was after the fifth or sixth whisky that Magnum showed up, and we shifted into our family's parallel universe.

I was surprised to see him in that bar of all bars. Whenever I meet him, it's on Saint-Jacques Street, near the stock exchange, where he dabbles without getting rich. I'm the one who picks up the cheque when we go out to eat. This little cave-like bar, long and drafty, where Tommy and I were sitting at a tiny table set in a recess in the wall, was a long way from the chrome bars he normally haunts.

Judging by his gait, he was smashed, and he was heading to the bathroom when he hesitated in front of our table.

'Hey! It's … it's Angèle!'

I wanted to make a joke to erase the mistake, but, in that brief hesitation, I had the revelation that had been waiting for me all those years. Before me, like a stone statue that comes to life and becomes human with the wave of a magic wand, I saw Tommy's face open up, start to shine, her features become smooth, her eyes light up, and on her lips I saw the caress of that smile, Angèle's soft smile, which made us believe, for a moment, that time had stood still and that she had come back to us. A moment of grace that evaporated as soon as Magnum made a move toward her.

'Hey, Ange … '

Tommy's eyes immediately darkened, all her features hardened, she became herself again, prickly, menacing, a wild beast crouched in rage, and Magnum, suddenly understanding his mistake, sunk into the chair where he had plunked himself down. Stone-cold sober.

For a moment I wondered whether Tommy had in fact become Angèle before our eyes, whether the gentle Angèle wasn't actually in hiding all these years under the features of Tommy the shrew, or whether, in the end, they were in fact interchangeable, one appearing at the other's will – or whether, more confusing still, they were really the same person. And while my mind rejected the idea of having been fooled, I saw myself back in Norco, a young boy of eight, nine at the most, a half-pint under the spell of the very same hallucination and menaced by the same fiery eyes. It was a recollection that had never bothered to surface in my memory.

Because it was indeed Tommy whom I had surprised in that dress with frills and flounces, all lace and silliness, a dazzling blue dress that danced around her legs. She was twirling and twirling, eyes closed, arms lifted to the sky, swept up in a reverie that was giving her wings, until, suddenly sensing a presence, she had opened her eyes and crashed headlong into mine.

'Angèle's getting carried away again in one of the McDougall dresses': that's exactly what I thought at the time. Strange how I can still remember what I thought, even though I can't remember what I said. Something harsh and hurtful, something worthy of Geronimo no doubt, because the McDougall dresses bothered us to no end.

Had Magnum also happened upon Tommy one day, dancing in a McDougall dress? As he made conversation with her in the dimly lit bar, did he have the vision of a little girl hiding behind the dynamite shed, or in the woods, or in a mine building, a little girl carefully taking off her boy's clothes and, after looking around, putting on a princess dress and stepping into a dream?

I watched him while he tried to carry on a normal conversation with Tommy, slumped in his chair, still dazed by the apparition of Angèle, and I wondered: have we all figured out at different times that Tommy could become Angèle?

That night stayed burned in my mind. The three of us at that little table at a bar whose name I don't know and that I couldn't find afterward, try as I might, as if it had appeared just for the delirium of that night, the three of us, Magnum, Tommy and me, our three solitudes brought together, three floating islands, three tectonic plates incapable of moving toward one another, each adrift in our own thoughts.

That night, the image of the half-smiling girl in the Studebaker was clouded forever more. I saw her outlined softly against the little hill in front of the house, floating as if on a screen warped by the heat. Émilien got behind the wheel; he had finished checking the car. Geronimo, who was beside him, sighed with relief. And in back, among the brown paper bags, I see Angèle's sensible little dress, I see her smooth hair, I see her gentle smile trying to form on her tensed lips, and I see Tommy, wracked with pain. At that point, she was the only one of the three of them who knew that Angèle had stayed at the bottom of the mine.

Do any of us still believe what we saw?

Since that night, I have been consumed by the need to find out what each person knows about that terrible day when Tommy stood in for Angèle.

I couldn't get anything out of Magnum. Every time I tried to take him back to that night in the little bar, he pretended to have forgotten everything: 'What a tear. Jesus, I was loaded!'

Once, I replied without thinking: 'It was quite a tear. You were so drunk, you thought Tommy was Angèle.'

His eyes flew open in surprise.

'You were even more drunk than I was.'

And then, softer: 'Don't try to pull that crap on me.'

The topic was closed forever. We never again discussed the night when Angèle appeared to us in the phantom bar.

As for Tommy, the reason I hunt her down from time to time at her retreat in the Great North isn't because I'm hoping for her to come clean. No, I use journalistic pretexts to show up at her home because I want to be there when she's not paying attention and Angèle's smile creeps onto her face.

In fact, no one has come clean. The day we lost Angèle in the mine is too locked down in our minds for it to pop up in a sudden twist of conversation.

But my quest has been the pretext to track down every member of the family, wherever they are, whether lost in the Andes or behind Chechen barricades. I tracked them all down, one by one, and I've kept up loose, on-again, off-again relationships with them so that no one will think anything of it.

Geronimo was the hardest to find. True to form, he isn't associated with a humanitarian organization; he funds his career as war surgeon through donations from anonymous rich people who deposit large sums in his Swiss bank account. That's what I finally found out after making the rounds of every aid organization on the planet. The first time I reached him by phone, he was as cold as a scalpel. He was in Afghanistan.

Émilien, on the other hand, was fairly easy to find. My letter went to four or five Australian towns before reaching Kalgoorlie, where he has made a new life for himself. We kept up an erratic correspondence, one that was innocuous, almost trivial, but pleasant. That's how one day I was able to bring up the image in the Studebaker under cover of small talk. 'Are you still into cars?' I asked him. And for a whole year, we discussed the relative merits of American and Japanese cars. 'Do you remember your old Studebaker, how it used to wheeze its way up hills?' To that, he answered that he had too many beaters in his life to remember them all. In my next letter, I said that I, on the contrary, had kept an indelible memory: 'Your old Studebaker was where I saw Geronimo and Angèle for the last time. Unless, correct me if I'm wrong, it was Tommy. They were so much alike.' His answer took months in coming and took on a whole other tone: 'That day, what was done was done for better or for worse, and you know full well who was in the car with us. Why do you want to make me say it?'

Whether with Yahoo, Big Yellow or the Weewuns, who were so young at the time of the accident, it was always the same thing. Once I would manage to bring up the image of the Studebaker, a brick wall would go up to stop all my questions dead.

The Old Maid was the least pliable of them all. You couldn't make the slightest allusion to the past without her starting to wail that there was nothing left in Norco but a house the wind whipped through, and that we should leave the memories to squabble amongst themselves. 'Nostalgia is a disease of the soul.' I don't believe a word she says. You just have to see her to know how attached she has stayed to the family. Ours, not hers, or rather any of hers, because she has had two or three husbands, many children, and they all left her once they figured out that her heart was too heavy for love.

She lives in a miserable little room over the kitchen of the Hôtel Caouette in Val-d'Or, alone, her heart blighted, feeling like the world will crumble if she drops her guard.

Her diviner's eye can spot Angèle's image the second it appears. I have tried different approaches, but every time the conversation brushes too closely against a family shadow, I see her rear up, all her senses on alert, eyes full of fury, and then suddenly she explodes about her boss, about her kids who are trying to get money out of her, about anything that will distract us from the image of Angèle, and I wait, because sometimes, after the storm, there are tears, and in between the sobs, she says something that gives me some insight into the burden of her responsibilities.

The Old Maid forced Tommy to get in the back seat of the Studebaker that day. I know it as surely as if she had told me. And my theory was confirmed as soon as their eyes met in the lobby of the Quatre-Temps.

They think I had always dreamed of Australia. The truth is that I couldn't take my family anymore.

Australia was a way of making them dream. I was the oldest, practically their father, because ours had turned into a rock zombie, and I was overwhelmed. I didn't have Geronimo's intelligence; I had nothing to impress them aside from my birthright. Australia was perfect. It wasn't the stifling civilization of Europe, it wasn't the plodding pace of a backward society, it wasn't our American cousins. It was so big and strange, an intergalactic place cast adrift in the middle of the Indian Ocean, a place you couldn't dream about without your heart wanting to burst with some combination of fear and joy.

In Norco, the dream was palpable. When I got home, I could see the talk my great continental explorer character would generate.

I didn't think I'd have to one day go through with it. Australia was just a vision, a mirage in the desolation of Norco, and then I dove into the sea of illusion. On August 17, 1965, I booked my flight, and two weeks later, I was on my way to Sydney. Before me lay the land down under, its Great Barrier Reef, its surfer beaches, its golden youth, its friendly smiles. Behind me lay the pain I wanted to shed. I was breaking free from my family.

I crisscrossed Australia searching for a place where I could rebuild my life, but wherever I was tempted to stop, familiar faces would rob the place of its gentleness and send me back on the road. When you're a Cardinal, you can't just give in to the beauty of rustling palm trees in the setting sun. You need a harsh, austere environment you can chafe against, one you can use to condemn those who have it easier. I walked away from the green hills of Tasmania, I fled the beaches and everything that had drawn me to Australia, and I headed for the interior, where the most inhospitable desert in the world awaited me. For five years, I laid waste to my heart trying to forget. I was one of those stockmen who go from ranch to ranch, a veritable armada of the desert, always moving and craving the intense, penetrating pleasures that took me to Kalgoorlie.

It wasn't the ladies of Hay Street who kept me in Kalgoorlie, but rather the feeling of coming home after many pointless detours.

No matter where they are in the world, mining towns all have a sense of urgency about them, probably because of the nearby pit. At the time, Kalgoorlie was coasting on the fumes of a glorious past that, in the tumult of the last century's gold rush, had left magnificent colonnade buildings and the hum of a single mine, Mount Charlotte. Both dignified and coarse, the town had a touch of antiquated despair that was seductive and that later made it a tourist destination. But around it, in Norseman, Kanowna, Broad Arrow, Leonora and Laverton, in those mining towns on the edge, is where you can really feel the fear of the void and the desire to dive into it – ghost towns, or nearly, surrounding Kalgoorlie, such that Norco came to meet me in my exile and made me understand the futility of my escape: no matter where in the world I go, I will always have Tommy's grief-twisted face to bring me back to the pain.

The nagging look on Tommy's face lists all the terrible things we are guilty of, me and all the others. Her face is white with dread, black with the impulse for revenge, it is screaming in pain and it reduces to ash the pleasures I try to steal from life. I can't escape her. No matter where I go, I know that Tommy is there waiting for me, in the back seat of my old Studebaker, and that from the depths of her soul she will howl, 'Why didn't you stop it from happening?'

It's the howl of my conscience. In fact, she didn't say a word until we reached the covered bridge. She was sunk in the back seat, surrounded by all the paper bags that held her things, and Geronimo and I had almost forgotten her, we were so preoccupied by the accident. It was the Old Maid who had forced us to take her.

'Angèle is going with you.'

'What do you mean, Angèle is going with us?'

'Angèle is going to Montreal with you, you heard me.'

The air was crackling with heat. It was one of those hot, dry days that I had grown to like.

I didn't pay attention to the Old Maid's mumbled explanations – 'studies … the McDougalls … international school' – because time was wasting. The accident had just happened, and the hicks would be reporting it to the police.

She slid into the car without me really seeing her. Would I have guessed? Would I have understood the barbarity of the deception if I had given her even the slightest glance? They looked so much alike. And yet they were so different. Tommy, our tomboy, and Angèle, the Foster Child, as she had been known since she'd heeded the call of the McDougalls. They even had the same little weasel-shaped face, the receding chin, the prominent cheekbones, the narrow forehead and the eyes rimmed with thick eyelashes, but you could tell at a glance that they didn't run on the same dreams.

In that moment, I was concerned only with the state of my radiator. We had five hundred miles to go under an apocalyptic sun, and I was wondering whether it would make it. I had seen Geronimo steal a worried glance at the temperature gauge.

'Did you get it fixed?'

'What do you think? I did it myself. I'm not going to let a mechanic touch my car.'

'Are you sure about your welding? If the gauge is anything to go by, it looks like there's a geyser in your rad.'

'If it makes you feel better, I have a box of pepper in my toolbox.'

'Pepper? Never heard of that.'

'It works. I've tried it and it works. You need to use a lot, of course. It's not like peppering a steak. But a box of pepper will hold you for a while.'

In a way, I was glad my old rad was giving us a pretext for conversation. Neither of us wanted to talk about what was really on our minds.

It was at the bend in the road, where it starts to climb a little before the covered bridge, that we remembered she was there. We heard the crinkle of paper, no doubt the bags she was moving, and then that voice, a voice that was neither Tommy's nor Angèle's, a deep, cavernous voice, a voice ripped from the pain, hurled at us, a voice that in my dreams chastises me for not having prevented the disaster.

She yelled, 'Stop!'

I braked as though my life depended on it.

She yelled again, 'Stop! I'm getting out here,' and already I knew Angèle couldn't summon that much authority. It was Tommy. I felt as though I were being sucked into the abyss. I parked the car at the bottom of the hill slowly and carefully, putting off the moment I would have to face the person sitting in the back.

Geronimo was turned toward the back seat, frozen, devastated, tormented, astonishment and horror alternating in his eyes, and Tommy – because there could be no more doubt, it was Tommy in Angèle's dress – Tommy had him locked in the force field of her black, intense stare. She let him see all of her pain, and as she pulled some pants and a shirt out of a bag, the clothes that would settle the question, she did not take her eyes off Geronimo, to tell him what I was starting to understand without a single word coming out of her mouth: 'Look at me. Look at my clothes. See what you've done. Angèle died in the mine. You killed Angèle.'

Geronimo pushed the idea away with all his might. No, no, no … he refused to believe it, he fought, he begged, No! But I could see that he had accepted responsibility for Angèle's death.

In my worst nightmares, it's Angèle who comes to accuse me – the Patriarch, the oldest – of having left her to her fate. She towers over me, her presence expanding to fill the space, leaving not even a crack, and, miserable little insect that I am, I look for some way to get away from her. I wake up hoarse, with a sweaty girl beside me, threatening to kick me in the balls if I don't stop screaming. But more often than not, it's Tommy who appears in the back seat. She's wearing the dress she had on then, a plain dress, flowered cotton with a shirt collar, Angèle's Sunday dress, and she looks into my soul. It is torture, pure and simple. The dream is merciless in how it haunts me. I know it will loosen its grip only when it has broken my resistance and when, exhausted and out of breath, I see myself running from the body in the rubble of the mine, running from those outstretched arms begging me for help, running from the young man I was, and when the nightmare gets to that point, I know I will see Tommy, triumphant in her pain in the back seat of the car, pulling a rustle of lace and silk from one of the bags, and, without taking her eyes off me, brandishing one of the McDougall dresses: 'Why didn't you do anything to stop this?'

I can't take my family anymore.

I got a room at the Nullabor Guest House in Kalgoorlie, hoping that women and booze would get the better of me. In my letters – because they ended up finding me – I told them I was prospecting in the area. The region, Goldfield as it's called, may have been turned inside out, but there are still fortunes made on a stroke of luck. Not that long ago, there was a new rush in the spoil heaps of the Golden Mile. Why shouldn't I be one of those tourist-slash-prospectors who stumble upon a nugget after a heavy rain? I also told them that I had a vineyard in Swan Valley, sailboats for rent in Freo, anything so that they would believe that I was bound to exile by the sacred ties of prosperity.

The Old Man would have been disappointed if he knew that I have turned into what he most despises: a gambler. He has always steered clear of luck – with luck returning the favour, because all his life he prospected a few feet away from it, except for the Norco zinc deposit – and he wouldn't want to hear that one of his sons was doing business with bookies. 'Ugh! Men with nothing but money on their minds.'

Derbies are serious stuff. And then there's blackjack, poker, roulette and bets made with just about anyone at the end of a bitter night. But what I really like is two-up. It's an Australian version of heads or tails, slightly more formalized than the version played elsewhere because you need a ringer (the referee) and a spinner (the one who holds the two coins on a small board) as well as ten or so men, sometimes fewer, sometimes more, ready to bet on how the coins will hit the floor. What I like are the few minutes while the ringer takes the stakes, which for me are a delicacy of suffering and delight, because during those few minutes, I'm in another state, a state of frenzied concentration, tense as tense can be, absorbed by the two coins on the small board, and I wait for them to talk to me: heads or tails.

I wait for that quiver of the eyelid that tells me that the coins are going to come up heads. A slight tremor, scarcely a shiver, barely a tightening of the skin, a flutter of the wings of a butterfly under my eyelid, and I know that both coins will fall heads up, no matter what twist the spinner gives them and what somersaults they perform in the air. It's a moment of red-hot intensity that's worth so much more than the money I win.

And if the little miracle doesn't happen, if I don't feel anything under my eyelid, it means that the will of the coins is to show their royal face, their shiny side, the one stamped with the effigy of the Queen of England, who is also their queen, or that they can't decide and will fall any which way. In which case I bet a token amount out of courtesy, mainly not to arouse suspicion. Gambling is serious business in this country, and two-up is thought to be a game you can't cheat in, another source of national pride. It's even played in the tony Burswood Casino in Perth.

I discovered that the coins have a will of their own a long time ago. Maybe that's the way it is for all objects, and you just have to tune into them to hear what they have to say. That would mean luck is not the result of the fickle law of chance, but that it comes from a state of total receptiveness to the object of our desire. I have tested this theory with roulette and other games, but either the mechanism was rigged or it was too complicated. I never managed to hear what they were telling me.

The first time, I thought I was hallucinating. I thought it was the Old Man speaking to me. An impromptu two-up had been thrown together in a pub, I don't remember which one, and naturally I was one of the players. I hoped to win thirty or forty dollars, no more. The game was lacking in spirit, and the bets were pretty tame.

I was getting ready to place mine when a young digger shouted, 'Hey, you, Canadian, can't you do better than that?'

It was one of those arrogant young prospectors who hang around town. The night before, I had stolen a girl off him.

'Can you do better?' I snapped back, showing him a hundred dollar bill.

I was thrilled. Finally a bit of action.

He pulled out a bill, I pulled out another. The stakes climbed to four hundred dollars, and that was when, as the bid climbed, I felt the presence of the coins. It was just a tingle at that point, a light twitch under my eyelid, but already I knew I should put all senses on alert so I wouldn't miss a thing. I remembered the Old Man saying to me, 'It's like a tickle, and then your eye starts to flutter like it has a life of its own.' He told me how he had decided to dig a trench in Lot 7 of what was still just a planned residential area. 'A trench two feet wide, twenty feet long and two feet deep. It was a sight to behold. Beautiful rock twinkling black and grey. Sphalerite at its best. I knew I had found something big.'

Until that day I had taken those tickles for the whimsy of a prospecting poet, but now I knew I had to trust them. I focused my energy on the two coins, and when I felt the shiver that heralded a flutter under my eyelid, I emptied my pockets of everything I had left.

'Another hundred and eighty and I'm the one who calls it.'

And without thinking I said, 'Kangaroos.'

I knew that the coins would come up tails, or kangaroos.

The Old Man had uncovered the gigantic zinc deposit that would give birth to Norcoville, and that evening, I went home with the winnings, a few hundred dollars at the most, but it was enough to convince me I was lucky in two-up.

Why didn't the Old Man do the same? Why hadn't he prospected at random, contenting himself with wandering the woods, just enjoying the birds chirping and the fresh air, waiting for his eyelid to flutter and point the way to a major mineral showing? Instead, he insisted on gridding his claims with the work ethic of an ant, counting his steps to measure the distance covered, noting in his notebook the orientation of streams and the slope of the land, inspecting the roots of plants he ripped from the ground, scrutinizing the banks of the streams, looking for the slightest clue that could lead him to an outcropping or a rocky point that he would carefully sound before taking a few samples with the cold chisel, precious manna that he brought back from his rounds and that occupied his evenings.

'You can't count on luck,' he'd say. 'She's a fickle thing who flits from man to man without ever really undressing.'

He was prospecting scientifically, he said. He had learned about it in a book, *The Prospector's Guide*, a small volume bound in oilcloth, its purplish reds streaked with long cracks darkened by sweat and dust. An old edition that heralded, with measured enthusiasm, the magnetometer and other magnetic and electric detection devices that left him scratching his head. It was his bible, his missal. He carried it with him wherever he went and sometimes even consulted it at the dinner table when doubt overcame him and he needed to put his mind at rest.

He was a man of letters more than a *coureur des bois.* Sometimes I went out with him, and I never saw him get distracted by a bird singing or a ray of sunshine through the leaves. He had a geological concept in mind that would give him no rest. It was a batholith, a diabase dyke or another rock formation of ancient times that he had made out on the maps and that he was pursuing tirelessly among the clues the ground offered. He was looking for lead, zinc, copper, nickel – but not gold. He didn't like gold.

'Too fickle, too unpredictable,' he'd say. 'You think you've found a vein and it's actually a veinlet that splits off into the rock in filaments fine like hair, and then *poof*, it disappears for good.'

What he preferred were erratic blocks, blocks ripped from the rock mass by glaciers, blocks you could stumble upon, by chance, while walking, without any clues to their presence. They would appear suddenly, one by one, several hundred feet apart, and he had to follow them like a latter-day Sherlock Holmes. I think he liked them because they forced him to picture another geological concept, imagine the path of the glacier, imagine the huge boulders carried along a hundred thousand years ago under the mammoth ice, and, most importantly, imagine the enormous deposit that awaited him in the distance, the mother rock, the rock that had been stripped and grated by the glacier, violated and abandoned, and that would reveal its secrets to him. I liked listening to him talk about these things.

He was so taciturn at home, but he was downright chatty in the forest. He talked at length about his quest, his problems and his worries, the worst of his torments being his inability to talk money effectively when it came time to sell his rights to land he had developed.

'Land that you walked, scratched, examined under a magnifying glass. Land that you wondered about constantly, even in your dreams at night, and that is gradually revealed to you, just you. You can't put a price on that. And yet you have to sell it.'

I collected these confidences with a sense of incredible privilege. I was about twelve when he took me out with him. I would have followed him to the ends of the earth. For all of us, our father was a hero, a man who, like Christopher Columbus or Jacques Cartier, had discovered a new world.

At the time, Norco was at the pinnacle of its glory. The mine was producing at full capacity, zinc was selling for sixteen cents a pound, there was money to burn, the hotels and the restaurants echoed with laughter and fights breaking out. There were crowds at the movies and in the schools, and at home, in the sprawling shambles that served as our fortress, we watched prosperity pass us by. From the youngest to the oldest – and lord knows there was no shortage of children in our house – we all had, deeply rooted in our consciousness, the conviction that our father was a hero because he had discovered the mine that had given birth to our town.

Had they really stolen it from him? Even at the time, I, who was the eldest and therefore should have been on the front lines of the war of contempt that was brewing in the madhouse where we lived, I left it to the others to stoke the hatred.

In Norco, Albert Cardinal was known as the man who discovered the mine, but when the subject came up, it was to pity him. Poor Cardinal! The poor bastard! I don't know how many times I heard that sort of remark before I understood that they were actually talking about our father. It took me even longer to understand that they weren't pitying him for his poverty, or for the preposterous house he had moved from Perron, or for the swarm of children who called it home. They pitied him for of his inability to profit from his luck. Poor Cardinal. Couldn't even get rich on a discovery that big.

And like our father, I let them talk because I knew that we were going to be fabulously wealthy one day. He had confided the details of the deal to me one night in the tent. We had spent the day chasing after a stream of rhyolite that had turned out to be nothing, and the evening was looking glum. A nasty little drizzle, an overcast, moonless sky, cold and the mosquitoes had driven us into the close dampness of our tent. Outside, our fire was slowly dying.

I never liked the idea of sleeping in a tent without a well-stoked fire to burn through the night and wait in the morning under the hot ashes.

I must have been grumpy because the Old Man, who was studying his maps by the light of his headlamp, lifted his head to me.

'Something wrong?'

I grumbled something about the rain and the day's long walk, and he smiled a little.

'Would you like to hear how we're going to get rich?'

So to cheer me up and restore my faith, like humming a lullaby to a child who is scared of the dark, he told me about his negotiations with Northern Consolidated.

They had offered him fifty thousand dollars. 'They put ten thousand on the table and told me that forty thousand more would be waiting for me at the bank the next morning if I signed that very night.'

In the close quarters of our tent, it was hard for me – and it's still hard today – to imagine that timid, cautious man, alone in front of three pointy-toothed sharks, with all that money spread out on the table like a threat. 'All that money and their eagerness to close the deal made me furious. The drill core had just shown assay value of 3.2 percent zinc and 1.1 ounces of silver. Not bad. But I knew there was a lot more than that.'

'You had your own tests?'

I was only twelve years old, but I knew enough from conversations with the Old Man to be surprised that an independent prospector would be able to pay for his own diamond drilling.

'No, but I knew … '

He paused for a long while, lingering on the memory of the three men he would stick it to. Or maybe he was thinking of the trench he had dug on the side of the mountain that had revealed beautiful white streaks furrowing deep into the rock. Our father's silences were filled with glorious thoughts.

'I knew what the deposit was worth.'

He had demanded five thousand dollars and three hundred thousand shares of Northern Consolidated.

'Three hundred thousand shares, which were worth a dollar each a few weeks later, and five dollars and twenty cents two months later. Can you imagine?'

The drilling had revealed incredible assay values and a deposit of enormous proportions, such that we would be rich, incredibly rich, rich beyond our wildest dreams, the day when, 'if we could sit tight,' our father would sell his shares.

He sat so tight that the shares were hardly worth the paper they were printed on when the price of zinc plummeted into the pit of high finance, and Northern Consolidated moved on to make its millions somewhere else.

I had run the numbers. At $5.20 a share, we were millionaires one and a half times over: we could have repainted the house and laid sod down around it. We could have each had our own bike, fishing rod and a new suit, and in the basement, beside the hundred pounds of potatoes, there would have been a limitless supply of chips, chocolate bars and strawberry Kik. When the share price climbed to $6.50, we could have had a bath with a shower in every corner of the house and a television in every room. We could then have considered an in-ground pool, twice the size of the church, blue as a postcard sky, and it could have been converted into a skating rink in winter, covered with a see-through dome that would slough off snow and be the centre of attention in Norco. At $8.00 a share, I had run out of things to dream of.

Millions awaited us. I didn't care about the knowing smiles or our abject poverty, because all it was going to take was 'the right time' to come, and all that money would start gushing.

This wild hope made me a dreamer, a boy isolated from the tempest that shook the house. Hostilities against the hicks had already started at the time. They were still minor skirmishes – battles waged in the schoolyard, snowball fights and other idle-young-warrior posturing – but at home, inside our fortress, there was a slow-burning rage I could do nothing about.

We were angry with everyone who had taken possession of the mine. Whether Northern Consolidated, a distant spectre in its Toronto offices, the poor miners, our neighbours, barely better off than us, or the others, petty merchants and their employees who had never set foot in the mine but who reaped the benefits of it, they were all duly and diligently held in contempt.

And even though I was the eldest, I couldn't lead the troops into battle, because I was waiting for the big payoff.

In the absence of a real leader, a triumvirate was formed of the most fervent, loudest voices: those of Mustang, Yahoo and Fakir. During those years of prosperity, they were the ones who stoked the muted, hate-filled grumbling in the madhouse. When the mine closed and despair took over Norco, they had already left home, as had I. I was driving a cab in Montreal, and so Geronimo took command of the war of desolation that would make the Cardinals the princes of a kingdom that no longer was.

Which meant that I was merely the honorary head of the family, real power having been seized by those more violent and aggressive than me.

Anyhow, no one remembers that I was the first to go with the Old Man on his prospecting rounds. In the annals of the family, the only true apprentice our father ever had was Geronimo, who is also thought to be his only confidante, even though I know for a fact that Geronimo's heedlessness worried the Old Man. 'That boy's heart pumps nitroglycerine,' he'd say.

I don't care about setting the historical record straight. I don't care about restoring my place in the family annals. The only memories that are truly precious to me, my only bits of solace, are those private moments with our father, beside the fire or sitting on a tree stump while he explained the faults in the earth's crust that fill with magma, the resinous sparkle of sphalerite or his money problems. What I liked more than anything was his discovery of the Norco deposit. The magical moment when, like a diviner senses the presence of water in his divining rod, he felt his eyelid flutter, 'just a tickle' – that was enough to convince him to dig a trench on the side of the mountain, because, he would say, 'if the rock's magnetism had stopped me dead at that exact spot and travelled through my entire body to make my eyelid flutter, it meant that below my feet was a deposit that defied the imagination.' Magnetism! He searched for no other explanation for the incredible luck that flowed through him.

He followed the glacial boulders to the base of the rounded mountain that overlooks Norco, brownish float that could indicate the presence of galena or sphalerite equally. 'It was hard to tell at that point given the weathering of the rock.' The rest is history. He dug that incredible trench, which revealed long streaks of pure zinc sulphide going deep into the bedrock. The story made the papers. The entire mining world and all of Norco knows it, but no one knows about the little miracle that made his eyelid flutter.

I wouldn't have betrayed his confidence for anything in the world. Our conversations were my only solace in Norco. Unlike the others, who have glorious memories of our youth, what I remember most is the joy of those conversations and how oppressive it was to be the eldest in the family.

When the price of zinc plummeted to six cents a pound, my first thought was for our father. I was twenty at the time. I had been living in Montreal for a while, and I was still waiting for the millions. The dreams I dreamed for my loved ones had changed quite a bit. I dreamed of a Cardinal dynasty: university educations and successful careers, one of us the prime minister, another a renowned scientist, and yet another – why not – a Nobel Prize winner. All of this perched comfortably atop our millions.

I heard the news on the radio in my taxi. Well before mourning my plans for our family, I thought of our father, of the shares that he cherished like pieces of eternity and that would deliver him to a harsh reality now that they were worthless. I dumped my passenger on St. Laurent Boulevard, an old woman wound in scarves, and I headed to Norco, convinced that my presence was required.

Norco was in shock. Northern Consolidated had done the deed nimbly. The miners got the announcement that the mine was closing at the same time as their final paycheque and were escorted to the office by gorillas brought in at great expense from Toronto in case revolt was brewing in the ranks. A padlocked barrier was placed in front of the office, and they were already bustling about loading archives and other precious assets into vans. The precautions were unnecessary; the miners, too stunned by the disaster to entertain ideas of rebellion, were hunched over oceans of beer.

It was night by the time I arrived in Norco, and from the small hill on the road that offers a sweeping view of our little town, I could hear the clucking of the women, flocking together in front of the two hotels, beating their breasts over the final paycheques.

At home, all hell had broken loose. Geronimo greeted me with a triumphant smile.

'Did you hear?'

They crowded around me before I could even take a step, and it fell to the loudest to recount the day's events.

The kitchen was overcrowded and couldn't hold everyone. People were jostling and tugging. They were slamming into each other to make room for themselves in the doorway that led to the living room and the bedrooms. No one was in bed in spite of the late hour. The Old Maid was there, a baby asleep in her arms, Tootsie I suppose, since the Caboose wasn't born yet. Hanging on to her legs were Wapiti and Nefertiti – I could never tell them apart. And in a corner, the Twins were hand in hand. The entire household was assembled for an all-night vigil.

'Tonight, the world is ours!'

They had decided to celebrate the closure of the mine with a huge bonfire behind the house. It was provocation, pure and simple. Provocation that was even more bitter for the people of Norco when the next day they discovered that the tires that had fuelled the Cardinal bonfire had come from their sheds.

'We'll show them, goddamn hicks! Let's burn some rubber.'

I didn't get a word in edgewise in the ensuing commotion. They were moving the bedlam outdoors: blankets, pillows, the living room sofa and provisions for the night – even the television, which they thought they could get going without the antenna. All under the confused orders of Tut and Magnum, who had taken charge of the operation.

I grabbed Big Yellow as he went by and asked him where the Old Man was.

'In the basement, as usual.'

As for the Old Lady, no point in asking. The door to her room was closed. She was sleeping that short, deep sleep that allowed her to haunt our nights.

As I headed down to the basement, I wondered what harrowing scene awaited me. During the long hours on the road, I hadn't stopped wondering about the state I would find our father in and how I would comfort him.

He was standing in front of his workbench, busy scratching samples, and he realized I was there only once I was beside him.

'You came,' he said with a half smile.

It was neither a question nor an expression of surprise. He was noting in amusement that I had given in to panic.

'So tell me why you came all this way.'

His strange good mood made me hope for a moment that all was not lost, that maybe he had had time to sell his shares before the debacle and that our millions were safe and sound.

In a confused account that I couldn't myself understand, I told him about my mad dash to Norco, the old woman in the turban who didn't want to get out of my cab, my worries and the idea both sudden and unhoped-for that was beating a drum in my mind.

'Forget the shares, son. They aren't worth a nickel – might as well be zero. We have better things to do than to worry about pieces of paper.'

He was looking at me with his mischievous little eyes, grinning from ear to ear, like a child with a trick up his sleeve.

'Forget the shares,' he said again in his voice that told of confidences to come. He gestured to the bottom stair while he settled in on a case of dynamite. 'Sit there and listen up. Listen carefully, because I'm not going to repeat it.'

And that's when he told me what first sounded like a fairy tale and then, as he told his story, I spotted all the perils, and all my responsibilities, but I didn't have even the tiniest clue as to the tragedy that awaited us at the end of the adventure.

His story took us back four years, to the opening of the mine, when he accompanied the president and the other officials of Northern Consolidated, who were taking a group of journalists on a tour. 'It was the first time I had gone underground. I had never seen the inside of a mine before.'

He had been invited as the mine's discoverer, and he had been forgotten as soon as the introductions were made, so he lagged behind the group, a bit dazed by the racket of the machines and how pitch-black it was, but happy to be left on his own. He was walking slowly. 'What impressed me was how clearly you can see things with a little light in that pitch blackness.' The beam of his headlamp sweeping the rock walls of the drift showed him the forms left on the rock by geological movements – faults, folds, slips and igneous intrusions – all things that up to that point had been revealed to him only parsimoniously. 'I could clearly follow the sphalerite stringers in the volcanic rock. It was definitely a saddle-shaped deposit like I had seen in my copy of *The Prospector's Guide*, but seeing it with my own eyes was different than picturing it when you're prospecting on the surface.'

He was on the main drift, about a hundred feet from the group, when it happened. He recognized the tingling sensation under his eyelid, and then it stopped suddenly. It was just a light pins-and-needles feeling that travelled over the eye, barely an itch, 'but I knew that when I moved closer to the wall of the drift, I would find what was making my eyelid quiver.' He approached the wall, trying to make out in the design of the rock what was so desperately trying to catch his attention. That was when he was overcome by a serious tremor. It was no longer a simple blinking of his eyes. His eyelids were beating the air like hummingbird wings, and a radiant force, 'a ball of fire,' travelled right through him. His entire body shook with a feverish tremble, and during those endless seconds when he thought he was dying, he had the revelation of a vein of gold-bearing quartz.

'A quartz vein in greenschist. I didn't see it like I can see you. It was clearer than that. It was as if I could see under your skin, inside the rock, like X-ray vision. I saw it all in an instant. First, the greenschist, which was very dark, and then the vein of quartz, whitish, fractured, unbelievably cracked and, in the fissures, granules of bright yellow, a sun-mustard yellow, you know what I mean: native gold, my boy, pure gold, more than you can imagine. The vein was so full of it that in places it was blinding.'

The description of that quartz vein put him in such a state that I no longer recognized him.

'I thought you didn't like gold.'

His eyes disappeared in a squint with his smile, and he told me, hammering out each word with a trembling voice: 'You didn't see what I saw. A vein like that is beyond your wildest dreams. But I saw it with my own eyes. A few feet from the wall, in the greenschist, long, wide and rich, by god! I don't like gold when it's cagey, but when it offers itself to you on a platter like that, you don't look a gift horse in the mouth.'

I would have rather not believed in that quartz vein. But his description, the detail with which he answered my questions about its location, its dimensions, its dip angle, its extent and, above all, his assurance that he would find it exactly where he had left it once he emerged from his trance and went to join the group, 'two hundred and fifty-five steps from the mine stope,' all of this meant that I saw it too, in the schistose gangue, running northeast, and in the milky white of the quartz, the gold specks shimmering, the twinkling hope in our father's eyes, that would take us into the most adventurous enterprise of our lives.

I knew that he would not let that gold go. He had hoped it would be discovered and the value of our shares would skyrocket. Now that the mine was closed, and they had proven that they were not up to the task of finding it, he believed that the gold was his as a matter of right.

There was nothing to say, nothing to do. He would go get that quartz vein. I discovered a man who was determined, driven, who was not afraid of the dangers of the mine, or the illegal nature of his enterprise. His voice had grown firmer, and as he was explaining how he would go about it, I felt as though the world were crumbling around me.

That night, I thought of running away.

I could smell the burnt rubber and hear the clamour of the Cardinal celebration through the small basement window. I knew that our father's project would sound like a call to arms for the family, swept up as they had been since birth in a war of hate, and that they would throw themselves headlong into this adventure.

Extracting the quartz vein meant a covert operation, but how would that work in such a small town? How would we muffle the sound of the dynamite? How would we prevent the hicks from wondering about our comings and goings around the mine? And the truck – because we would need a truck – how would we get a truck? And more worrisome still, the gold, how would we sell it, and to whom?

All I wanted was to go straight back to Montreal, forget that I had almost stepped into this quagmire, start over, under a new name, with a new personality. But I knew full well that I would do nothing of the sort.

When I think back to that night, what I remember most is the acrid smell of the smoke, combined with the muddy funk of the basement. It was as if that oppressive odour contained the weight of my responsibilities. As if, that night, the fire had already taken over our lives. Fire and devastation: the ravaging heart of the fire and the desolation of burnt land. Norco was filled with the smell of something burning.

The summer that followed the closing of the mine was the most scorching. And the siege of devastation that had started under Geronimo's rule continued during the five years we exploited the mine in secret.

I would arrive from Montreal, the car overflowing with things the Old Man had asked me to buy, and well before the hill that led to the covered bridge, my nostrils would be filled with the sinuous smells of the fire that was raging against a cabin or along a corridor of wild grass, behind which ran a band of Cardinals young and old.

Geronimo was a little punk, twelve at the most, when he turned his attentions to what was called the siege of fire. He always impressed me. It doesn't surprise me that today he spends his time around the major battles raging in the world. He loves confrontation. He loves extreme tension. In Norco, he was a one-man army of liberation and oppression.

It was his skill with dynamite that earned him a job as our father's apprentice at the mine. In the plans that the Old Man and I came up with, that night when everything changed, we had initially chosen Magnum and Tut. They were fourteen and fifteen at the time, 'strong enough,' the Old Man had said, 'to turn the drill steel while the other hits it with the sledgehammer.' Because this was how he planned to extract the quartz from the surrounding shale. In actual fact, they often had to resort to dynamite, because while schist is weak rock, particularly argillite schist, they encountered tougher structures that refused to give up to the carbide bit of the drill steel. So they restricted themselves to a half stick of dynamite and avoided clear days when the sound of the blast would carry.

It took Geronimo only a year to replace Tut and Magnum. One day I arrived and it was done. Tut and Magnum were champing at the bit at home, and Geronimo was leaving in the morning with the Old Man, officially for the mining properties along the river – a ruse that fooled only the hicks, because, apart from the youngest, Wapiti, Nefertiti, Tootsie and particularly the young, feeble Caboose, who were always kept in the dark, we all knew that prospecting activities behind the mountain were just an alibi for our comings and goings from the mine.

My heart clenched when I learned who the Old Man had taken on as his apprentice. It was pique and jealousy mainly, because I could imagine their conversations in the damp dark of the mine. The clandestine nature of the task, the hostile environment of the abandoned mine, the constant danger of a rockfall or poorly controlled blasting – all that brings two people closer than years of drinking together. Particularly given that mining as imagined by the Old Man – artisanal in the extreme – required constant collaboration. It involved notching the rock to serrate it, first the green shale and then the quartz. The quartz vein was tabular in shape, two feet by four feet of beautiful white opalescence streaked with gold, and rose northwest over a dip of forty-five degrees, such that it had to be followed in a tunnel with just enough room for two men, a jackleg drill and a compressor. Every operation in such a restricted space required reflection and inventiveness, with no margin for error. More than anything I worried about the seductive appeal of Geronimo's intelligence in such conditions.

I rarely went to the mine in the five years after we took it over. My role in the affair, while important, kept me away. I was always on the road. I had given up driving the taxi to become a sales rep for Mines & Mills Supplies, a company that sold mining supplies. Aside from the advantages for our own procurement, my job put me in contact with mine managers, which gave me a way to discreetly sell our gold. The Old Man and I talked about it at length during that fateful night in the basement, and we had come up with a solution: finding a small gold mine and a less-than-scrupulous manager who, to supplement his ore and drive up the stock price, would agree to buy our gold on the QT. And this is why the small used truck we bought came down the mountain every evening, engine and headlights off, bringing a ton of our beautiful gold-studded quartz to the Goldstream Mine.

All these precautions couldn't keep the hicks in the dark about our activities indefinitely. Norco had changed a lot since it was abandoned by Northern Consolidated. It was no longer just a pack of poor people searching for themselves. They hadn't managed to build a life somewhere else or hadn't even considered it, and they stayed, lost in a town that was blighted by lack of hope, like those miserable wretches I sometimes see emerge into the oppressive heat of the afternoon at the Australian goldfield.

They loathed us as passionately as we loathed them. The siege of fire had reduced them to a hateful, dark, impotent mass that held back its venom, just waiting for the heavens to intervene and bring them justice. There were only a few of them left, a dozen families maybe, slinking along in fear of new troubles, victims of a reign of terror they had acquiesced to, and they watched us from their windows.

It never occurred to us that they would report us. We held them too firmly in our grip, we thought, for a sudden fit of dignity to make them that bold. 'I dare them,' Geronimo would say. 'Let them try and say just one word out of line ... '

I wasn't part of the war of harassment waged against the hicks all those years. My position as the eldest, thank god, exempted me from such displays of power, which I had no inclination for. Even Geronimo had to give them up. He was too old to beat on snot-nosed kids and run around chasing grass fires. But he still enjoyed the cruel games, and he was the one who instigated the most inspired of them.

He had become the family's leader. The uncontested, indisputable leader. With Tut and Magnum gone, he was now the oldest, if you didn't count the Old Maid – who, despite her twenty-two years and her indispensible presence, was still a girl – and if you didn't count me. I had put myself second under the weight of my responsibilities. I was just the faithful courier who could be counted on for the dynamite, the gas and the tools needed to exploit the mine. I came and went, I appeared and disappeared, always on the road, in a state of perpetual anxiety about what was waiting for me at home. I was worried about what might happen at the mine, an accident, the police; I was worried that one day I would see the Old Man in handcuffs, worried about our mother, who had withdrawn into unintelligible muttering since the birth of the Caboose, since she was no longer making babies, worried about what more Geronimo might have come up with. Who would be his victim this time? Tintin? El Toro? Or poor Angèle, whom he was constantly hounding?

Tintin was his lieutenant, his right-hand man. He was the one who was burning and subjugating Norco on his behalf, and he was the one Geronimo would turn on most often. Tintin accepted the humiliations and mistreatment with the self-denial of a knight facing an initiation rite.

But he turned his attentions to Angèle when she came home from the convent, or worse, from the McDougalls'. Angèle was a funny little girl. She had grown up with hopes that wilted in the dump we lived in. She was always looking for an escape, but she always came back to us, fresh as a rose, light and smiling, until Geronimo would resume plucking off her wings.

There was a surgical precision to his strikes. He knew exactly where to hit. In Angèle's case, it was barely tolerable cruelty. She had never been slapped, knocked about, beaten, or anything like that. Aside from Tommy, who gave as good as she got, the Cardinal girls were never in physical jeopardy at home. No, the treatment Geronimo reserved for Angèle was particularly nasty. Like forcing her, when she came back from the convent, wearing a white blouse and a spotless tunic, to count the cats rotting in a barrel behind the house in preparation for the infamous festival of cats, when the Cardinal clan paraded down the town's deserted streets with the poor things impaled on stakes. After she had counted the carcasses in the barrel, he would ask, 'Do we have enough?' and she had to figure out the number that would keep her from having to go back there, somewhere between the number deemed satisfactory and what there was in the barrel. 'You've forgotten that we need some for your guardian angel too, Sister Angèle.' She would go back to the barrel. 'And how many is that in Latin?' When the others no longer found the game funny or once he'd tired of it himself, he'd say in a disgusted tone, 'Go change. You smell like dead cat.' She would stay there, utterly helpless, her uniform dirty, standing in the middle of the living room, until Tommy would grab her by the sleeve and lead her to a bedroom.

I never got used to the look in her eye at those times, or rather the blank look in her eye. Her eyes staring and wide open with effort. She was waiting for the end of the ordeal, taking refuge somewhere inside herself, where pain meets the soul. Joan of Arc at the stake.

Would I have changed the course of events if I had found the strength to stand up to Geronimo?

I was twenty-five at the time. I was a man, and he was just a kid, sixteen or seventeen, his body barely out of adolescence, arms and legs flapping around him like panicked animals, his face spotted with acne, but grit in his muscles, a fierce look in his eye and a determination to terrorize. I was under his power, like the others.

No one stood up to him, not even the Old Man. He made himself invisible. We didn't even see him at meals anymore.

You had to watch to catch a glimpse before he fled from the table down into the basement. And Geronimo, later in the evening, after sitting enthroned in the living room and dispensing sarcasm and smacks to whomever he wanted, would then go down the stairs to the basement. The murmur of their conversation would chill my heart. It was hearing them that made me start to dream of Australia.

All I could find to salvage my dignity was that miserable dream. The dream – not something I had to commit to at first, a fantasy barely taken shape in my mind, the illusion of a departure that was supposed to give my presence more value – was only a dream, a hoax, a smokescreen meant to mask my powerlessness. I never really believed in it until the day I had to face the fact that I no longer had access to our father's private world. It was Geronimo he confided in now.

I had become the quiet force you turn to when a job needed doing. I was the one they asked to take Bibi for an abortion when she got pregnant. Poor Bibi. She cried all the way to Montreal. And I was the one they turned to when we had to get the image of Angèle alive out of Norco.

But I wasn't the right man for the job anymore. I understood that when I arrived one day and found Geronimo and the Old Man in conversation in the basement in the middle of the afternoon. They hadn't gone to the mine that day. In fact, they hadn't been all week.

A plane had flown over Norco at the beginning of the week, slowly and at low altitude, trailing a device that left no doubt about what we had to fear. Airborne geophysics had started to get results in the North, particularly in the Matagami area. It was new at the time, so when the plane flew over Norco, everyone rushed to see it, and well after it was out of sight, the hicks were still in the streets, jumping and waving for the pilot to turn back and pass his instrument over the mountain again.

'You should have seen them. Hicker than ever!'

I hadn't even gotten to the house when the Old Maid starting telling me the whole story.

I had no trouble imagining the hope this flyover generated among the hicks. Their insidious hatred would grow stronger now that there was hope that 'their' mine would be returned to them. Because that was indeed what it was about. The reopening of the mine. Modern geophysics wouldn't miss a super-rich gold quartz vein that our father, with no resources other than his prospector's luck, had seen twinkling through the rock. So we had to expect that in a few weeks or a few months, a team of geologists would land in Norco to study the anomaly detected by the plane's thingamajig and find out what had been going on.

The house was on red alert. The Old Maid and anyone mature enough to grasp the situation were watching me with a worried eye.

And of course, my first reaction was to ask where the Old Man was.

When they told me he was with Geronimo, I hesitated before heading down to the basement. That hadn't been my territory for a long time. But I couldn't help myself, it was an old reflex. I felt as though he needed me, given the circumstances.

I was wrong. Bitter disappointment awaited me.

They were sitting on empty boxes of dynamite, facing one another, bodies hunched in a position that showed only their rounded backs, bent over the dirt floor, absorbed in the silences of their conversation, and once they heard me on the stairs, they raised their heads at the same time, looked at me as if I had appeared from another world, and the Old Man said, 'Wait upstairs, Émilien. We'll be up in a minute.'

He might as well have slapped me across the face.

In the days, weeks and months that followed – because the matter was only resolved in July with the explosion at the mine, our final blast, the one that took Angèle – I withdrew into sullen solitude, the only stance that would leave me with a shred of dignity, which no one noticed because the house was in such a dither. We were on red alert; there was constant tension, day and night. The house was on tenterhooks.

We had never considered the possibility of the mine reopening, and now that the possibility was real, all too real, we had to hurry to hide any trace of our activities. Geronimo and Tintin went to retrieve our supplies, burning on site whatever couldn't be transported at night, because the hicks had grown bolder and were keeping a close eye on us. But we all knew that these precautions would be pointless once they discovered our tunnel and, at the end of a thousand feet of sweat and black night, the sparkle of the quartz vein.

The Old Man and Geronimo would lock themselves in the basement for hours on end, and when they came out, we would look for the glint of the beginnings of a solution in their eyes, but hiding a thousand-foot hole in the rock is like moving a mountain. It was a lost cause, and we knew it. And I, who no longer hoped for anything, except maybe a glance from our father, waited in my corner and, after a time, I would grab my windbreaker in a huff and throw myself into long solitary walks through the streets of Norco. I would come back home only once I had drunk my fill of bitterness, and I could show my everyday face to the family in the living room.

Who knows what was said during those weeks and months in the basement. Who can tell whether the solution was decided by joint agreement or whether Geronimo took it upon himself to blast the mine, without breathing a word to our father.

The day before the explosion, we celebrated Pester's birthday. The tension had reached its pinnacle. The Old Man had just learned that Northern Consolidated had recovered its rights to the mine. It was now called New Northern Consolidated and was preparing to send in a team of geologists. All of this he had learned in Val-d'Or, in Amos, at the Department of Mines and in the bars he had started to haunt. He needn't have taken the trouble; the rumour had spread to Norco on its own steam. The hicks had emerged from their burrows, and the winds of vengeance were blowing.

In front of the house, on our hill, six vehicles were parked helter-skelter, all old beaters, except for Yahoo's Rambler. We were all there, alerted by the news, worried about what would happen, sombre, tense, armed with the high spirits of warriors to celebrate Pester's eleventh birthday. Our last family gathering.

Late in the evening, or during the night, I don't know anymore – time has become confused, it was perhaps only in the morning that I noticed – Geronimo disappeared. He spent the evening in the living room with us, in the middle of the three-seater sofa, in the middle of the discussions that we loved. The discussion that night sailed on a raging sea. We railed against the forces of the universe, against the very idea of God, and, in slightly quieter tones, in the trough of the wave, we grumbled about New Northern Consolidated wanting to take over our mine. As the storm led us to wonder once more how we could save our family's honour, Geronimo let a long silence linger in the foam of the wave and then, looking at us one after the other, puffing himself up with an air of triumph as the authority of his gaze made its way around the living room, he finally smiled and in a slow, decided voice, he said: 'Smymine.'

The next day, when we saw the dust raised by the collapse of the mine, we knew what his mission had been.

I took him to Montreal, along with the image of Angèle dying under tons of rock.

It was only later, when I realized I couldn't live with that image anymore, that Australia became the only choice. I booked my flight, but before I could disappear into exile forever, I had to see whether I had any hope of finding what I had lost. I went back to Norco.

The house was suspended in a state of unreality. No one seemed to be truly there. And when I went down to the basement, the Old Man didn't seem to understand what I was doing there.

How do you live with eyes boring into your soul, accusing you of killing your sister?

I knew that in agreeing to come to the prospectors' conference I would have to brave those eyes. The eyes of Tommy and all the others, shoulder to shoulder in their pain. My karma awaited me.

I still don't know what made me accept. When El Toro called me in Grozny, I could have just told him that I couldn't leave, that my presence was required, which was in fact the truth, since fighting had resumed pretty much everywhere. On the border of Dagestan, in Gudermes, in Argun, and even in Achkhoy-Martan. There had been a lull in July, after the ceasefire agreement, but since Dudayev had distanced himself from Imayev, peace was no longer in the cards. Flesh ravaged by Kalashnikovs and rocket launchers gave me no rest.

And yet here I am, here, in this low-rent luxury hotel, exposed to the eyes of my loved ones, unable to take a step in the magma of emotion, dizzy to the point of vertigo with all the familiar faces and voices. Here I am at the finish line after running for so many years. Here is Geronimo standing before his loved ones, no weapons or defences, completely powerless, like the child he never was.

I recognized them all. Even the Caboose. Although he is now a man, he still harbours within him the worried, admiring little boy who ran between our legs and who was sent off with a cuff, but who would always come back, relentless as a fly, until he could find protection with one of us, usually Tintin.

He hasn't stopped buzzing around me since I walked through the doors of the hotel.

All it took was a moment; I had barely set foot in the lobby, and I felt the earth shift in my stomach. A sense of imminent, intimate danger went through me like a knife. The threat closed in as the minutes and the seconds ticked slowly by. What in the world am I doing in this bad dream?

El Toro was the first to spot me. He waved to me from where he stood, and then he came toward me, all smiles, his hand outstretched, confident, voice booming, as if he were the host of this reunion. The others approached slowly, and I found myself at the centre of an uneasy vibe, everyone trying to avoid eye contact with everyone else. Tommy hadn't made her entrance yet, but I knew that with me there, we were just waiting for her arrival to set the drama in motion.

I almost didn't recognize her. She had aged, like all of us, but more so, in a way that revealed nothing of what she had been. When I saw a woman creep toward the front desk, I thought it was a chambermaid come to collect her pay, a poor old woman broken by life. But her clothes weren't shabby. She wore a parka, too warm for the season, trimmed with white fox, black pants with a neat crease in the front, short boots and a red plaid shirt, a flame in the opening of the parka. Her clothes were inappropriate, but they weren't cheap, or dirty, or worn. It was her bearing, bent, hunched over herself, that created the impression of a wretched life spent escaping any appearance of opulence.

In the lobby, El Toro's voice rang out: 'There's Tommy!' Even then, I couldn't quite believe it was her dark, closed face.

It was only once Tommy crossed paths with the Old Maid that I recognized her. Her body straightened up with the savage pride of an animal, all her features lit up and, in spite of the wrinkles, in spite of all the years, in spite of the fear that gripped my heart, I saw Tommy's black eyes bore into the Old Maid, eyes that have never stopped haunting me, accusing me of having killed Angèle.

Tommy had left her land in the North, and she had us all in her sights. Particularly me. She wouldn't forgive me anything. Not Angèle's death, not the McDougall dresses, not the Latin sessions in the living room. I would be spared nothing of what I had done or said. Wordlessly, with only the force of her eyes, just like in Émilien's car after the explosion at the mine, when I thought I was merely escaping the hicks and their thirst for vengeance, and she bayonetted me with her dark eyes and showed me Angèle buried under the tons of rock that I had just blasted.

How can I explain what happened that day without breaking the fine thread of lies that keeps us all in equilibrium? Everyone thought I was the one who blew up the mine. I was the only person responsible for Angèle's death. And that's the way it should be. There is no point in two of us being under the glaring lights of accusation.

That day I knew I was leaving Norco forever. The hicks weren't going to miss a perfect opportunity for revenge for everything we had put them through. I didn't know it then, but in running from the police – their inquiries would inevitably turn to us – I had to run from my family as well.

All I wanted was to destroy any trace of our activities at the mine. The Old Man and I had discussed it at length, and no clear solution had presented itself. Blasting was considered, but immediately rejected. 'Too dangerous,' the Old Man had said. I had proposed the idea of dynamiting the central pillar of the mine stope, a column of rock about twenty feet in diameter, rising over sixty feet to the ceiling of the enormous room dug in the centre of the mountain, the heart of the mine. 'It's way too dangerous. If you blow up that pillar, the entire mine will collapse. And you'll be at the centre of the explosion. You'll be swallowed whole.'

'And what if we blast on the east side? If we blew up the pillar at the entrance to the drift that leads to our tunnel? The east lateral pillar?'

It was still too dangerous. He would turn himself in to the police shackled hand and foot rather than see his children risk their lives in an operation that involved too much dynamite and too much rock. Sometimes his cautiousness was exasperating.

Having drilled from every angle, I knew how to blow up the lateral pillar without killing myself.

At night during the week, I transported the dynamite and fuses we needed to the mine, with Tintin, who was my accomplice of the hour. Tintin had earned his name. He was always running to the rescue of the small and the vulnerable. He protected widows and orphans, specifically the Weewuns, the Caboose and sometimes even Angèle when he saw her on the verge of collapsing under the weight of a trial, but when put to the test, he was the first to leap into the fray, the first to sneer at foolishness and fear. He was my most faithful right-hand man in the war we were waging to take back our rights. He was naïve, but with a sense of duty that never wavered.

He was the one who had helped me remove our equipment from the mine in the weeks before. And now, we were undoing everything we had done. We were bringing back the drill, the compressor and the explosives, and we were starting to drill blast holes at the base of the east lateral pillar.

I had to explain why.

I should have been wary of the kid's questions. He quickly understood that by blowing up the lateral pillar, I was intending to obstruct the drift and, with a bit of luck, the entrance to our tunnel. But what interested him, like me a few weeks earlier, was the central pillar, an all-out blast, the complete collapse of the mine, an explosion that would attack the stone structure of the mine and would leave only a miserable pile of rocks at the bottom of a crater, an indiscriminate hole from which neither another mine nor evidence of our activities could be extracted. And just as I had done with the Old Man, he peppered me with questions.

I understood later, much later, that my answers to his questions were what helped him figure out what dynamite charge to set in the middle of the shaft (which is what he did, the poor guy) for the force of the two explosions, his and mine, to meet in a single blast and tear down the central pillar, resulting in the explosion that we both wanted, a huge and terrible detonation that shook the depths of the earth, at once exploding, lifting and rupturing the mountain's bare summit, which collapsed in an unspeakable din, the rocks splitting, smashing together, crashing together, the thunder of their fall to the bottom of the gaping hole of the mine, the creaking of the mother rock cleaving from all directions, a trembling I felt beneath my feet. The combined force of our two blasts shattered the internal structure of the mine and struck the very foundations of the rock on which it rested. It was more than we could have hoped for, beyond all expectations, a complete victory. And I savoured the glory of this victory, not knowing that Tintin, on the other face of the mountain, was hurrying to join me.

I heard a final convulsion of the mountain, a muffled and deep explosion, and I hastily brushed the dust from my clothes because I knew full well that the explosion would attract the horde of hicks and that I would have to face them.

I posted myself behind a mine building to watch their arrival, and that's where I was when I saw Tintin appear. He was covered in dust and sweat, out of breath from running, but he was beaming with pride. I didn't understand.

'What are you doing here?'

He smiled a wide, triumphant smile in response. He was bursting with pride, and he was staring at me, his eyes shining, searching for complicity in mine. I didn't want to understand.

'For Christ's sake, what are you doing here?'

I can see us there, me, an idiot lusting for glory that I refused to share, unable to face facts, and him, Tintin, a brash young kid in awe of his exploit, claiming his share of the praise. I was torn between what I needed to understand and the smack that would recalibrate his emotions. And then the hicks arrived, and I knew what I had to do.

They came at top speed, the men, the women, the children, an undistinguishable mass, stunned, dazed, addled by some inkling of the disaster, and they crowded around the crater, contemplating their misfortune in silence and, when their wits returned, when they had formed a vague idea of what might have happened, they retreated to the mine office, saying my name, 'Geronimo! Where's Geronimo?' I knew then that no matter what happened, there had to be only one guilty party to offer them, because the vengeance of the weak can be a terrible thing indeed.

I grabbed Tintin and I said, looking him straight in the eye so that my words would sink into every fibre of his being, 'Only one person is to blame for this and that's me. You stay here and don't show your face until you're cleaned up.'

I thank god for the inspiration I had at that moment when he was getting ready to climb up on the mountain and show himself to them. Neither of us knew at that point that Angèle was at the bottom of the mine. I was just trying to protect him from the fury of the hicks. And I'm glad that I had the good sense to lift a burden from him that he wouldn't have been able to bear. He didn't have what it takes. He was everything you could hope for in a Cardinal, but deep inside him lay great sensitivity, too great for me to have let him shoulder the blame for Angèle's death.

I told him again when we met up years later: 'Only one person is to blame, and that's me.'

Tintin is a gentle soul. He wouldn't have survived if I hadn't taken full responsibility for what happened that day. How could he have? I was older, tougher, harder, and the only way I managed to live with the burden was by sinking deeper into the carnage, massacres and internecine wars, which dwarf my soul under a pain that is greater than mine. A war surgeon. I didn't choose a career, I didn't choose to be a hero, I simply buried myself in a pain that wasn't my own. It was the only instinct of survival that I had left after Tommy's black eyes bore into my heart and showed me Angèle, my sister, my favourite sister in spite of what people may think – Angèle, the strongest, the most intelligent, the best one of all of us – Angèle, her body crushed under tons of rock.

She was the most brilliant of us all. She could have done our name proud if we had let her live. She was twenty-four-carat Cardinal, but so unpredictable, so puzzling. How could she be interested in the mathematics of imaginary numbers and baubles at the same time?

I know everyone thought I was hard on her. No one really understood, except her, maybe. I was trying to get closer to that secret part of her. I wanted to shake her so that she would reveal herself and show us what was so alluring about such pointless desires: dresses, trinkets, good manners, all that fool's gold that drew her like a bee to honey. She let herself be abused. She accepted the trials with an abandon that moved me every time. And her gentleness …

She was an enigma. I never stopped wondering about her from the moment she let herself be seduced by the McDougalls' fancy clothes and mansion. None of us would have been caught in such an artless trap. The little girl with the light heart came and went, one foot in our world and the other in a dream. She went away regularly to play princess at the McDougalls' and came back to us just as regularly, beaming in her doll's dresses, whirling and twirling, as if she didn't know that we were going to burst her bubble to bring her back to the fold. Returning from her jaunts was difficult, and yet she always ended up leaving again. She would go back to the McDougalls' with a persistent lightheartedness every summer, even if every time the reception that awaited her when she came home was more of an ordeal. I could never understand what attracted her to them.

I thought she was doing it as a challenge, because sometimes I would catch a look in her eye, at the worst part of an ordeal, a look that showed me just how strong she was and humiliated me. I could never say exactly what it was. But I know that it was that hard core that I was after in her.

We never had real conversations. She was three years younger than me, a superfluous girl, and I was destined to become head of the household.

Only once could we have had a real conversation, and I blew it, even though I was the one who had wanted to be alone with her. It was on a Sunday afternoon, at the mine. I asked her to come with me, under the pretext of having forgotten a magnifying glass that the Old Man urgently needed. The others smelled a rat. She was in her school uniform, a navy blue tunic and a white blouse, and they were all convinced that I had something special in store for her.

She impressed me. She had learned English at the McDougalls', Latin with the nuns, was interested in ancient civilizations and modern mathematics, and she had managed to keep her place in the household in spite of the life she was leading somewhere else. She was sixteen and would soon be off to another world without me having put my finger on whatever burned deep in her soul. I had decided to approach her softly. I wanted her to want to open up to me. But I was pretty unpolished at the time, and I didn't know how to handle intimate conversations.

I thought I would take advantage of the Sunday lull. We lived on top of each other at home, intertwined, stuck together, constantly fighting for a tiny bit of space, in spite of the maze of bedrooms and kitchen/living rooms that gave us a great deal of it. But on Sunday, peace broke out, a sort of languor settled over the house, and we scattered here and there, on the porch with a book, in a bedroom chasing shadows on the walls, and we watched time go by. I thought I would take advantage of the hush to quietly ask her to come with me. I hadn't banked on the interest the slightest initiative of the great Geronimo would generate.

She was with Tommy in the last bedroom upstairs and, from the tone of their voices, I knew they were sharing confidences. Tommy dug in her heels as soon as she saw me in the doorway. And rather than the friendly approach I had prepared, I heard myself saying, 'Before you wear your eyes out over your Latin textbooks, come help me find the magnifying glass the Old Man lost at the mine.'

There was nothing I could do. The commotion that my appearance in the bedroom had caused and the harshness of my words had raised the dust in the house. The shockwave moved from room to room, disrupting the idleness of our Sunday afternoon with the turbulence the news caused: 'Geronimo is taking Angèle to the mine!'

We had gone through the kitchen/living rooms on the second floor, followed by faces that each lit up in turn with the excitement of the news. Angèle was tensed with the pain of not knowing what awaited her – it would be something new because she had never gone to the mine – and I was hurrying to hide my annoyance. At one end of the second floor, frozen in a rectangle of light that was its sole source of illumination, was Tommy, impotent in her rage.

I had hoped that at the mine, in what had become my world – because I went there to split rock every day with the Old

Man – I could start a casual, friendly conversation about what we were doing and gently get a closer look at her soul. I was counting on the blackness at the bottom of the mine and that strange silence that penetrated your entire being and left you feeling vulnerable, an impression I had myself when I went there for the first time.

You entered the mine via a ramp dug into the mountainside, and daylight dimmed as you went deeper into what was nothing more than a roadway, just large enough to accommodate three men of medium build walking side by side. It led to the mine stope. It was there that I hoped to get the truth from Angèle, in the enormous room carved in the rock. The silence was more enveloping than in other parts, and the darkness was thicker. At the centre of this underground cathedral, there was a precise point where a voice, bouncing off the rocky ridges left between the many pillars that supported the vault, came back in a series of echoes, becoming superhuman. I had experienced it a number of times, and it had left me shaken.

Angèle remained immune to the echo of my voice. We were in what I call the main nave of the cathedral, and I was explaining the ingenious system of arches and pillars that distributed the weight of thousands of tons of rock above our heads. The beam from my flashlight roamed the rock walls, disappeared into the cavernous depths, came back to us on another pillar and sometimes, when I abruptly changed direction, a beam of light would illuminate Angèle's tensed face. She stayed beside me, ramrod straight, the picture of pride, waiting for the torment to begin or end, because she was convinced that I had brought her there for a new bit of torture and didn't understand what all the staging was about.

I couldn't get a word out of her the whole time we were in the mine stope. It was only later, in the tunnel, after climbing a thousand feet of ladders that led to our quartz vein, that I felt her tension start to ebb.

The place was impressive, it must be said, for anyone who had never been there. A tiny cubbyhole, barely large enough to accommodate the two of us, flanked on either side by dizzying drops, one serving as an ore chute and the other as a means of access. And above us, embedded in the shale, the quartz vein. It was an apparition of blinding white surrounded by darkness.

I don't know if it was the strangeness of the place, her interest in the quartz vein or the budding conviction that I meant her no harm, had no dirty tricks up my sleeve ... but I felt Angèle's resistance fade.

I spoke in a soft voice so as not to extinguish the faint glimmer of trust that held out for true intimacy. She was listening carefully and, little by little, she started asking questions. About our blasting technique, about how we disposed of the barren rock and, of course, about the quartz vein.

She was struck by the fact that we extracted six ounces of gold from a ton of rock.

'All this for six lousy ounces of gold?'

I tried to get her to see the error in her thinking.

'Six ounces a ton is an incredible assay value. Even the Old Man has never seen or heard of that sort of assay. We extract a ton a day, six ounces of gold a day. Imagine what that makes at the end of the year, at thirty-five bucks an ounce!'

'And what do you do with the gold?'

'Well, we sell it to ... Okay, we sell it to a guy. He's the manager of a mine, a little gold mine that's not doing so well. The guy isn't too worried about the hows and the whys, and he buys our gold at, let's say, twenty bucks an ounce because none of this is legit.'

'No, I mean, in the end, what's all that gold used for?'

'Well, it's used to make bracelets, necklaces, all kinds of jewellery, gilding for statues, gold teeth ... '

'So … ' (and here she deliberately emphasized the words), 'fool's gold, basically.'

I was gobsmacked. Caught completely off-guard. I should have been furious, but I was too impressed by her intelligence to contemplate revenge. Luckily there were no witnesses to the affront.

I pretended to discover the magnifying glass that I had left the day before behind a pile of rocks, and I said in a tone meant to reassert my authority: 'Let's go.'

I swear that I didn't even think about the tunic and the white blouse. It was when we got home and I saw the car belonging to the parents of a school friend who made a detour by Norco to take Angèle back to the convent that I realized. Her tunic was covered with black, sticky dust, and the only part of the white blouse that was still white were the buttons.

They were waiting for us. The school friend and her parents in their car, doors closed and windows rolled up in spite of the late-afternoon heat, all smiling with the same exaggerated patience and stealing furtive glances at the surrounding desolation. And on the porch was a noisy assembly of the Cardinal tribe, making a show of looking the intruders right in the eye.

Angèle went to meet her humiliation as a queen would go to the gallows. Straight and serene in her soiled uniform, without a shadow of annoyance on her face, she walked slowly toward the car, giving the audience all the time it needed to admire the damage, and she got in the back seat, beside her school friend, whose horrified face offered a taste of the commotion that the soiled uniform would create at the convent.

The humiliation was beyond tolerable. She could have taken the time to change in the house and come back with a clean uniform, but no. She chose to embrace the humiliation and force us to look at the disgrace that awaited one of our own at the detested temple of the convent. No one on the porch was in the mood for rejoicing. And standing apart from them, I could only admire her incredible strength of character once again.

I stopped wanting to drag the secrets of her soul from her. I was wounded deep inside. She had snubbed the hand I held out to her and, more importantly, she had made my life seem absurd – mine, our father's, Émilien's, everyone's – because extracting the quartz vein was the family business, and our gold the most glorious tribute of war that we had squeezed out of Norco. I couldn't watch it be dragged through the mire of fool's gold.

I'll admit that the tortures that awaited Angèle when she returned from the convent became pure vengeance on my part. But there was no glory, because she took refuge inside herself, leaving nothing on the surface but a smooth image on which we could read our own disarray.

Angèle's strength lay in her ability to reach us where we didn't expect it. I understood that later in talking to Tintin.

Tintin is the only person in whom I confide emotions that are eating away at me. He has become a sort of monk. He lives with his four or five children at the end of a country road. No wife and no hope other than to watch his children grow.

When I left Norco, I thought I would never go back. I hadn't anticipated that the need to grate my soul against our past would force me to return. I go every two or three years now, only in summer, because the road that leads there is impassable in the winter, and for hours I fill my heart with every form of suffering imaginable. The Norco air, the land defenceless under the sun, the smell of warm grass, the gusts of cool air that start from an opening in the forest and whip over the cruellest memories of the past, and, smack in the middle of my line of sight, the house, our poor, big house, awaits me. I do my whole routine: I lean into the most powerful images, I wind and unwind the thread, I strangle myself, I stab myself, I slit my throat, I annihilate myself, I exterminate myself, and once I'm dead, when I feel nothing left inside me but the bottom of the dizzying pit of pain, I get back in the car and I drive along a dusty maze of country roads until I reach Tintin's place.

I didn't know that my wandering would lead to Tintin's the first time I went back to Norco. I was just back from a mission in Chad. My first mission for the Red Cross. Plenty of others followed, to Chad and other places, to the point that I could no longer stomach reporting to the humanitarian bureaucracy at the pulpit in Geneva. I'm a lone ranger now, exasperating the close-knit international community of boy scouts.

After Chad, the crush of refugee camps, the overpopulated streets of N'Djamena, and then Europe, I needed wide-open spaces, I needed to feel the bracing air of freedom. After landing at the airport in Montreal, I rented a car and took Highway 117 without thinking.

It seems that the barbarity of the internecine wars where I tend to others' wounds have only made my own wounds worse, because as I drive this road, past the inhabited area of the Laurentians, past Mont Laurier, once the air tingles with the bracing smell of pines, once the sky opens up over vast stretches of calm water and my soul wants to go off to meet this grandeur, once it smells the northern air and hears the call of wide-open spaces, my soul clenches, because it knows what's waiting for it at the end of the road.

That time, I didn't know what awaited me. I hadn't been back to Norco in twenty years. The road was taking me there without my knowing it.

Things hadn't changed much. You could see that prosperity had passed through, but very quickly, and in fits and starts, leaving the towns and the villages with a few new homes, looking proud, facades redone, lawns closely shorn, and, not very far off, a few miles away, in a notch in the forest, a hovel in fake brick, surrounded by horrible bric-a-brac that delighted me, because it was the image I had taken with me and that I was finally revisiting, the image of a man living alone or with a wife as forlorn as him, a few kids perhaps, a dog, a gun, obvious, unselfconscious poverty, a life that defies all the laws of this world.

When I arrived at the side road I knew so well, I realized that Norco no longer existed. The road was just a thin ribbon of dirt, with long yellow grass growing at its centre, leaving two uneven ruts on either side that I was driving in. It was when I spotted the covered bridge at the bend in the winding road that descends slowly toward the river that I knew that I was going to meet my pain. From the other side of the bridge, there was that spot, burned in my memory, where Tommy's black eyes came crashing down on me. 'Look, look at me, look at what you've done.' I crossed the bridge slowly because of the planks that had come loose from the deck and the voice that pursued me. 'Look where your sick games have led.' Coming out of the half-light of the covered bridge, I saw us, Émilien, Tommy and me, out in the sun, out in the nightmare, in Émilien's old car. 'Look at her carefully. Listen to her scream. See all those tons of rock raining down on her. Look at her flesh tearing, the blood splattering, her stomach splitting open, her brain exploding. Look what you've done. You've killed Angèle.'

'Noooooooo!'

I was the one screaming in horror. The vision I was being forced to look at was too horrible. My entire being was rejecting it, while simultaneously trying to feed on it, to wallow in the abomination to reach the peak of the pain. I saw Angéle dying in a pool of her blood. I saw the mound of flesh and organs. I replayed the scene from the beginning, from when the scream started to the unrecognizable body, torn open, eviscerated, ground under tons and tons of rock, and I started over. Salvation was to be found only in torture.

Tommy got out of the car, taking with her the pants and shirt that would put an end to the horrible charade. We knew from that moment on, Émilien and I, that she had taken charge of saving the family. Or that she had been put in charge of it. We waited for her while she went behind a thicket to take off Angèle's dress, her flowered Sunday dress, and put on the pants and the shirt that would hide the death, my blame and our family's vulnerability forever.

As she gave me back the dress, she said, 'I never want to see you again.'

She headed back to Norco, with her slow, purposeful step, and I followed her fading image, wondering whether other visions awaited me and whether I would survive.

There were still a few houses standing. Ours and the Laroses', the Morins' and the Desrosiers', I think. Over the years, I have seen these houses go downhill. Every visit, one more has fallen down and yet another will finally lie down to rest once the weight of the winter is upon it. Only our house was still truly standing, with its old companion, the dynamite shed, at its side.

This time I was able to go into the house. The porch and the outside stairs could still hold me. I went through every room, I opened the cupboard doors in the four kitchen/living rooms. I searched everywhere, brushing aside spiderwebs, chasing mice that had made their nests in whatever had been left behind – broken box springs, piles of boxes, nameless clothing and objects – but when I wanted to go down into the basement, my heart couldn't take it anymore. I had exhausted all my suffering. I stood before the big black hole in front of me, unable either to take the step that would have sent me headlong into it or to step back from muddled contemplation of what I could make out from the faint ray of drowsy light coming from the small basement window: on the dirt floor, blocks of cement and the debris of the stairs, and on the west wall, our father's workbench, above which dangled boards that had served as shelves.

I don't remember leaving the house: I only remember finding myself lying stretched out on the mountainside and the long cry that escaped from my throat.

I must have driven there because when I got up, I saw the car below. I could see the glint of the metal in the sun through the brush that had taken over the road to the mine.

I could taste blood and tears in my throat, and I had the impression of having broken all my limbs in hand-to-hand combat with an invisible force. I was overwhelmed, completely panicked by the idea of having lost consciousness for all this time. The rental car that sparkled in the sun seemed like my life buoy.

I fled Norco without looking back and without asking where this moment of madness would take me, content to just press down on the accelerator, not thinking of anything except getting as far away from there as possible. I took the little road to avoid the covered bridge, for fear of meeting Tommy's ghost again, and I drove at full tilt along the forbidding, isolated country roads that seemed to be leading me nowhere.

The first houses started to pop up after I felt I had returned a little to the living, but I didn't recognize the people, the houses or even the road. I realized I had gotten lost in the land where I was born. 'Lost in hick territory,' I said to myself, knowing the joke was on me.

I took the car down the back roads that crisscrossed, bifurcated, petered out in a long dusty series and all wound up looking alike, and I ended up where my frenzied escape was supposed to take me.

The house had sad, black tarpaper as siding that gaped in great swaths open to the elements. Small and square, with no stylish touches, not even a stoop in front of the door, it seemed to have sprung up from the dirt like the humblest forest mushroom and didn't care what people thought of it, in the shade of the tall willow trees that surrounded it. Pretty much everywhere between the trees, sheds spilled their guts onto the grass, and there were the cheerful cries of children, the sweet little face of one of them astonished by my presence, and then another, more boldly contemplating the stranger behind the wheel of the car that had stopped, and finally the dog, barking like a little soldier.

I had stopped there, attracted by the pleasant image and the far-off echo it awoke within me, not knowing that this was where I would find the haven my soul so desperately needed, but mainly because the house was at the end of a road, in a cul-de-sac, and I was forced to interrupt my race.

'Dad, someone's here ... '

The man was splitting wood in front of a shed, and he looked in my direction a long time before setting down his axe to approach me.

At what point did I feel Tintin's radiant presence in this dark, heavy man? He was moving toward me with a step that grew more and more hesitant as he approached the car, and, when he leaned on the door, there was an instant when both of us, at the same time, moved toward one another even before we could say who this man was extending his hand and grinning from ear to ear.

We stayed that way, frozen in that incredible handshake, unable to tear ourselves apart, until the whining of the children who were playing around us brought us back to the here and now. Then there was a long moment of hesitation. We had to say something, greet each other in some way, but the words stayed stuck in our throats, intimidated by the grace of the moment. I felt the need to break the silence, at the same time as I wanted to prolong the pure beauty of the emotion that united us, and in the end I found no better greeting than: 'How's the Old Lady?'

And he, just as tongue-tied, answered, 'Come on in. We'll have a beer.'

That's how I entered my brother Tintin's world, a strange world, filled with children laughing and making faces, a world where he was at ease, used to the pleasures of a quiet life and the rough surface of a broken soul. He lived in this charming little house under the willows with his four or five kids – he himself didn't keep track of which ones he had fathered and which ones had been left behind. 'I could never figure women out. They come, they settle in, and before you can say *phew!* they're gone again.' He lived from a little prospecting, chopping wood and trapping. 'The children take care of the rest,' he said, gesturing to the mess in the kitchen.

We talked for hours. About his life, about mine, about what had become of this one or that one, about Norco. There had been an investigation after the explosion. Police had come to question everyone and had left with tons of clues but not a single ounce of evidence against us. The town crumbled soon after. The hicks realized that there was no future for them there, and they left one by one, taking their houses with them if they were up to the journey or leaving them behind. 'We stopped burning things. There was no point anymore. And anyway, we had to keep something for ourselves. There was virtually nothing left.'

'And the Old Man?'

Our father had gone back to prospecting. He was no luckier than before, and he didn't discover anything, but he had gone back to being a prospector. He had found his soul again. Did he know what had happened to Angèle? Yes, he knew. I didn't need to ask Tintin. I could guess from his way of avoiding the topic that Angèle's death had weighed on the whole family. 'Nothing was ever the same after that.' He repeated it I don't know how many times.

It seems only the Caboose lived through those dark days unscathed. 'A happy guy.' Pretty soon, only he and the Old Maid were left at home with our parents. Norco was being dismantled. The two hotels were removed from their foundations, placed on huge semis and hauled away to continue their slovenly lives somewhere else. The church became the Hurault parish hall, and the schools were torn down brick by brick. Once they found themselves alone on their island, the Old Man agreed to weigh anchor.

'You can't imagine how many baskets of rocks we brought up from the basement!'

Tintin's big booming laugh erased the vision I was creating of our father's heartrending goodbyes to his town. I pictured him, the poor man, on the little hill where our house stood, overseeing the move, making sure that none of his rock samples got lost in all the hauling. Alone in his thoughts, in spite of all the bustle around him, he saw his town, the town he had given birth to, sinking into what would soon be a shapeless pile of memories. Did he take one last look at the mine? Did he have a final thought for Angèle?

Tintin's story was punctuated by those big, good-natured laughs, strange in so solemn a man, and they lightened up the conversation. He had barely launched into one of these bursts of hilarity, when I saw him sneak an inquisitive look at me.

'Did you go back? Is that where you're coming from?'

I described what I had seen without telling him what happened to me.

'And do you go back from time to time?'

'No, never.'

We both knew what his refusal meant.

'You're not to blame ... ' I began.

I wanted to continue. I wanted to explain to him, but there was a vast continent between us that we hadn't yet crossed. We would have to wait for other meetings before our souls would be ready to hear what had to be said.

We talked more for hours still. The kids – some of them pretty big – made dinner. And it was only once the first shadows of the night appeared that I realized that I would have to leave my brother's cozy little house, where I already felt I had made a nest.

We could only talk about the innocuous: the hicks, the war, politics and religion, inspiring the same disgusted contempt as before. We went back to the way we were, two brothers, two Cardinals whom life had separated and who got their backs up as one. And when it came time to say goodbye, I thought that we would do it the Cardinal way, with no fuss, a smart remark at the ready in case of any sign of emotion, and a firm handshake.

Tintin waited until I was in my car, probably because he wasn't expecting an answer to his question. The engine was already running, and he popped his head through the window, his face close to mine, and he asked me, as if all day and all night there had been only this question on the tips of our tongues: 'Do you know what she was doing there?'

I didn't know what Angèle was doing at the mine that day. I didn't have the foggiest idea, and the fact that Tintin asked the question meant that no one knew. Her secret died with her. I left knowing that I would be back, that I couldn't resist the temptation to come and explore the enigma of Angèle with the only one of my brothers with whom I could speak freely. Over the years, his little house would become the place where I could lay down my pain.

The shimmering of the sun on the sheet metal roofs of his sheds is a sure guide. Once I see the flashes of light between the willows, I am again drawn in by the image that made me stop the first time. Tintin built his sheds like our father did.

The next time we saw each other, he told me, 'Once they didn't need me anymore, I stopped going back to Norco. I settled here, right nearby, well before the Old Man decided to leave Norco. I was their handyman. They needed someone. There was nothing left in town. And now, there are all these kids … '

He wouldn't go to Norco, but as soon as he started waiting for me to come, he began maintaining the covered bridge. I recognized the invisible hand that replaced the planks on the deck, solidified the joists and repaired the rafters. He would wait for me from one year to the next, and if the violence kept me on the other side of the world for too long or if my heart refused to go beat itself up in Norco and my visits were a few years apart, I knew it was a long wait. 'I thought you were dead somewhere off in one of your wars,' he would say, half-mocking, half-serious, as he opened the door.

I didn't have any more visions. Tommy no longer appeared to me at the bend at the covered bridge. Angèle's presence was the only one I could feel, under the mountain where I went to run aground, lying on my side, listening for a moan, a confession. For Christ's sake, what were you doing there? Why did you have to be there? Silence. The mountain keeps her secret and I die, I scream, I tear my heart out.

I try to postpone the moment when I find myself on the mountain. I wander along what used to be paved, lit roads, now no more than tracks with thin strips of asphalt. I go from house to house, from one pile of debris to another. I search among the dried-up cattails for the spot where we would go trout fishing. I look for a place where a pleasant memory can surface, and I spend a long time in front of our house.

Since my first visit, the outdoor stairs have collapsed, and the kitchen floor has caved in. I don't dare go in anymore. Under the enchantment of my memories, I would like to see Big Yellow and his pirate's mop of hair. I want to see Matma, so inappropriately named. I want to see Zorro. But they are just battered memories, images with blurry lines, whereas what awaits me under the mountain is flesh and blood.

– 144 –

Most of all I want to see our mother. She is old now and still just as lost in her muddled thoughts. Tintin paints a sad picture of her. I can't imagine her in an overheated bungalow, no children around her, cooking for faceless mouths, volunteers who come to get the enormous concoctions she feels compelled to prepare and that end up on the plates of the destitute.

I can't believe that after all this time she doesn't know what happened.

How could a woman like her not feel in her flesh that she was missing a child? How could she not have heard Angèle's heartrending cry under the avalanche of rocks? How could Angèle's absence after all these years stifle that cry? In spite of how tired she was from all of those children born one after the other, our mother was there for every one of us. I know it, because I would wait for the delicious moment when her eyes would settle on me, at the table when she would serve dinner and count her children, at night when she went from bed to bed and, oh, the joy of it, I felt her lean over my day's worries. I know that she knew every nook and cranny of my soul. How could Angèle have hidden her death from her?

That was how I wanted Norco to return my mother to me. Pretty, nonchalant, half-dozing at the foot of the bed where I waited for her, the weight of the day lifted from her shoulders, possibly happy. That is the image I try to rekindle.

'Why don't you go see her?'

All I had to do was to stop at Val-d'Or, go to Rue des Trembles, near the shopping centre, and ring the doorbell. The Old Lady would open her arms wide to me. 'And what about the Old Man, Tintin? Or hasn't he occurred to you?'

'What about the Old Man?'

The Old Man would have known in no time what happened at the mine. We thought he was lost in his dreams, impervious to the noise of the house, completely crazed in his obsession with rocks, but I know that his intuition was sharp and that he managed his dynamite with the care of a bank teller. I found that out at my expense when I took a stick of dynamite from him for my number in front of that girl (what was her name again?) who was getting in the way of my romance with the beautiful Nicole with the gypsy eyes.

'The time you made the principal's boobs shake?'

Tintin was too young at the time to truly remember the story, but it had been told to him so often that he knew all the details, except no one knew the finale, not even the Old Maid, in spite of her importance in our house.

The end of the story is that the stick of dynamite I had carried against my chest all day had made me sick, and the Old Man knew it when he came up to the bedroom where I was holding my head in my hands. 'It's the nitroglycerine,' he said to me in a sickly sweet tone that sounded more sarcastic than he intended. 'The humidity had been at the stick you took. Didn't you notice that the paper was stained, like by big drops of oil? That's the nitroglycerine that seeped through the wax paper and gave you that headache. If you can't tell bad dynamite from good, my boy, you don't touch it.'

'He knew I had stolen a stick from the dynamite shed, one stick! And he knew which one. He practically had it nicknamed.'

'And you think … '

'I don't think, I know. He's a lot more clever than people give him credit for. With just a little chitchat, without batting an eye, he would stitch me up good, and without my even realizing what was going on, we would have ended up talking about the explosion, and I would have answered his questions. He would have known the exact number of sticks of dynamite I had used, would have been able to tell them from the ones left in the shed, and he would have figured out the rest.'

'So that's why you never went back to see him, so he wouldn't know I was with you that day?'

'Listen to me: I'm the one who decided to blow up the mine. I'm the one who's to blame for what happened that day. Me alone. There's no point in two of us having to shoulder that responsibility.'

When we get to that point, to the blame I refuse to share, Tintin's eyes grow wide and get glassy with anger.

'I'm not some little shit you can lead around by the nose anymore. You can't keep telling me what to think and what not to think. Your controlling will never end.'

Seeing him so unhappy, I sometimes tell myself that we should have let the truth come out. I would have gone to prison, Tintin probably too. Maybe we would have shared a cell, and we would be out by now. We would have atoned for what we did together, and together we would have asked for Angèle's forgiveness. That would have been better than the solitude, me running from war to war in the distant hope of a stray bullet, him having retreated deep into his land, cultivating poverty and self-denial, and the others, El Toro, Magnum, the Old Maid, Tommy, their lives not much better. And what about the Caboose, the poor kid who vaguely knows that a secret has slipped by him and who goes from sibling to sibling, searching for a past that has been kept hidden? Could we have forged a bit of peace and happiness for ourselves if we had agreed to live out our tragedy in the light of day?

'Our family was never looking for happiness. So we can't resent never finding any.'

Tintin's observations are disarmingly lucid. Living like he does at the end of the road, his only company children, who ask him for nothing or so little – bread on the table and the freedom to run through the fields – he has had plenty of time to think and sort through his thoughts.

'You know, poverty is freedom. When you don't have to fight for wealth and power, all that's left is what you need, and that's plenty to fill a life.'

'And what do you see from on high in your poor man's nirvana?'

'I can see that we messed up our hearts and our minds.'

'Meaning?'

'Meaning that it's about time that you release me.'

We had this conversation during my last visit, just two months ago.

We have been meeting this way, periodically and with the same intensity, for the past ten years, and I had created a somewhat idyllic image of my brother lost and found, free of any ties, poor, 'majestically poor' says the Caboose, who is still in awe of the days when we were the kings of Norco, which he tries to rediscover in Tintin's stubborn silence.

'The others come to see me from time to time too, and they all get that same look when they see how poor I am. It's as if I were the keeper of something that's precious to them. My being poor isn't a sort of pride or self-denial. I just don't know how to live.'

I too had admired Tintin's poverty. Until I realized that he was deeply unhappy. Because of me. Because of the silence that I forced on him. Because his soul had remained a prisoner as long as I refused him the right to share the blame for Angèle's death.

We left each other with gloom in our hearts. Before leaving, I muttered to him what I had said so many times and which, I could tell, was no longer enough.

'It's enough that there's one guilty party. There's nothing to be gained by pointing the finger at each other.'

And he said, sadder than ever, 'Still with your grand ideas. The Great Geronimo who roams the big old world with a heavy sorrow that he can't lay down, revelling in his battle honours. What would you do without that as a defence?'

I went back to Grozny. Dudyev had just rejected the disarmament agreement. The separatist camp was divided. Twenty-odd injured men awaited me. I went back to my scalpel.

And then I got the call from El Toro.

I still don't quite know why I came to this conference. After the unsettling reunions, we found ourselves in a strange, unreal place, no one quite knowing how to find a new balance in the whirl of emotions. We sought each other out in the crowd of geologists and prospectors in ties, thinking we were avoiding one another. Groups of Cardinals formed and dissipated like sand dunes in the wind. And Tintin trailed around the halls, an unhappy fellow, waiting for me to give him back his share of the truth.

Truth is not where we think it is.

I tell myself that if it weren't for that fateful Sunday I brought Angèle to the mine, she wouldn't have known how to get there. She'd still be alive today.

This conference is a one giant battle. I don't know which is hardest, holding my rage in check or curbing the turmoil that is straining to break free. And then there is stoking the pleasure of watching them squirm in my presence. How can I want all this at the same time when nearby, our mother's tired eyes keep making the rounds of her brood searching for a truth that escapes her?

It's the second day of the conference. They will be presenting the Prospector Emeritus medal to our father in a few moments, and the ordeal will be over. I can go back to where I came from, back to sweet silence. Here, words are as sharp as rock. I've grown unaccustomed to conversations that riddle you with pointless words.

They have put us all in an anteroom adjoining the big room where the ceremony will take place. This is a surprise. No one ever mentioned us getting on stage with our father when they award the medal.

'It's too good to be true,' the guy from the Prospectors Association explained. 'It's the first time one of our honorees has shown up with his whole family. It's too good a chance to miss. Such a big family! It's going to make a great photo.'

The guy has no idea of the hell he has condemned us to behind those closed doors.

For the sake of the photo and the perpetuity of their archives, we would just have to put up with our thoughts hurtling into one another. The room is not all that small. There is plenty of space for us to move among the chairs set out in no particular order, to get away from the beginnings of a conversation and the thick silences to one of the fake leather chairs taking on airs at the back of the room, and then to get up and pretend that we are contemplating the landscapes hanging on the wall or the thick pine forest through the picture windows running along the opposite wall. But time drags on, thoughts are screaming impatiently. When will they come to let us out of this room?

Our mother is the only one who manages to escape the torment. She is sitting quietly on a straight-backed chair in the centre of the room, and she is not moving an eyelash. It's as if she is asleep. Her hands are clasped, lost in the folds of her dress, a horrible purple polka dot thing, no doubt the brainchild of the Old Maid, who is wearing the same colours. Her hair is done in a complicated chignon, and you can see her bare pink scalp under the fine furrows of grey hair. It's hard to look at. She looks like a baby bird left out in the rain, practically naked under the thin threads of down plastered along its coarse-grained skin. From time to time, the chignon comes to life, moves left to right, right to left, and our mother looks blankly around the room. She is exhausted.

The Old Man is by her side. Or rather he is by the side of the pedestal ashtray, the only one in the room. He is chain-smoking. I don't know whether it's the ceremony or the ambient anxiety that is making him nervous.

Ever since the conference began, he hasn't stopped saying that this medal is bullshit, a joke invented for canoe prospectors. He also calls them sightseers and day-trippers, and he can't stand them. They are the prospectors who paddle daintily along lakes and rivers, shading their eyes with their hands, looking for a spot to pitch their tent for the night and prospect a little, in places they have already camped and prospected, in single file like ducks in a brood. The freshwater idle. Whereas he is a backcountry prospector.

'Yes, but what exactly is the medal for?'

He has let his sons rib him for the past two days.

'If it's for the Norco deposit, you should tell them that a posthumous medal would have been just fine.'

We always held accolades in contempt, so now that we are all gathered for one of these shows of public vanity, we have to find an honourable way to distance ourselves from it.

Mocking and joking about the medal helps pass the time without stirring things up. There is no drama, no settling of accounts, no fuss, nothing but heavy silence and sidelong glances.

The medal would help us survive our thoughts. The jokes start again. Big Yellow cracks the first one.

'Getting a medal is just the beginning. You have to find a place for it in your basement. You'll have to tidy up your rock collection.'

'You'll have to frame it, build an altar to it, give it pride of place. That medal has been blessed by the president of the Prospectors Association himself.'

'Let us kneel before the Prospector Emeritus. *Ora pro nobis, miserere* and *tutti quanti.* The mass has begun.'

The Old Man gives us a shy smile. He likes his sons' swaggering insolence. He tries to answer in the same tone, but he doesn't quite know how.

'So will you tell us why they're giving you this medal?'

A mischievous look flashes in his eyes and he says: 'You may not believe me, but … it's for having prospected a few feet away from luck.'

He knows that we criticize him when he isn't there, affectionately perhaps, but still in an accusatory tone, of having a pickaxe that was more dreamer than diviner of riches. We don't want nice clothes or other vanities any more than he does, but we would have liked to win now and again. We would have liked to have seen him come home from his claims at night and proudly announce that he had just discovered an incredible deposit. Instead, all he had to offer was his fatigue and hope for tomorrow. We used to say that he was prospecting a few feet away from luck. We didn't think that he knew about it.

It is a quiet victory over his children's insolence, and he savours it by smiling till wrinkles form around his eyes.

'I prospected a few feet away from luck all my life,' he says, smiling even wider. 'It's a lot truer than you think. All my life, aside from the Norco deposit, but that's another story, all my life, I prospected where the vein started.'

Hearing the reedy singsong of our father's voice is always an event in our lives. He says so little. His voice becomes animated only around mining people.

So, to hear him make a speech that looks like it is going to be long and full draws us toward him, in the centre of the room. Even me, who has avoided making possibly compromising contact during the conference, I leave my observation post in front of one of the windows and join the small crowd that has gathered around our parents. Magnum and Yahoo part to make room for me.

'Yes, my whole life. Everyone knew. Word spread. Cardinal has a gift for finding the tail ends of veins, they said. They rushed to register claims next to mine at the Department of Mines. It wasn't long before I would see them arrive with their devil's gear.'

I can feel Geronimo's angry breath on the back of my neck. He can't bear the idea of someone taking advantage of our father. He is right behind me, and I feel him getting more agitated as the story unfolds.

'They would set up on the edge of my claims, with all their prospecting paraphernalia. As for me, I would follow a clue I had found just by studying the land and imagining what it would be like underground. Nothing in my hands, everything in my head. And I had it, the vein! First, a little yellow line in a veinlet of quartz, two hundred feet farther, another outcrop, the fine line got wider, started to show glints of rainbow, chalcopyrite for sure, a copper deposit that was taking form, and I would follow it for weeks, using my shovel, my pickaxe and my dynamite, until the vein revealed itself, and I got to the limit of my claims, where those bastard gizmo prospectors were waiting for me so that they would know where to start their work.'

The gizmo prospectors are the ones who run around the woods with magnetometers, flowmeters, gravimeters and other modern inventions. Our father's enemies. In the heyday of his anger, he called them gizmographers.

'They stole all your discoveries from you?'

El Toro's question stirs up an old hatred. It moves through our little crowd but doesn't reach me. I have bigger grudges.

'*Stole* is not the word they would use. They bought my claims. At a price that, well … '

As he explains the ins and outs of the transactions, I look at our mother, numb from fatigue on her ugly straight-backed chair, but still aware of what is going on around her. Watching her carefully, I notice that she reacts to our father's words. She has an almost tender way of nodding her head at every point he makes.

He explains that they would pay him for the rights to his claims with shares in the mine, and that's how he became a shareholder in all those companies that built assets from veins that he handed over to them. Some of them are extending the tentacles of their empire in South America and Africa.

'The medal is a form of recognition,' he says.

'For having prospected a few feet away from luck,' Pester adds, with a touch of bitterness.

Opinions are divided on what to think. Magnum, to my left, is excited to hear that our father has all that wealth within reach. Yahoo thinks he's being had again. Émilien is just worried.

'You still haven't sold your shares?'

We understand from our father's sardonic grin that those shares are private victories that he likes to savour in secret and so he has guarded them closely.

As for me, I have no opinion. I didn't come here to talk about money.

Standing beside our mother, the Caboose follows the debate without taking his eyes off me. He has been under my feet since the beginning of the conference. He won't stop hovering around me, wondering why I'm here. Poor Caboose. The poor kid was denied the truth and is running around in circles, getting tangled up in his questions.

I can sense, however, that he is coming to a decision. His eyes have stopped on something, an idea that emboldens him and prompts him to address me.

'What about you, Angèle, what do you think?'

He is petrified by his daring. He doesn't dare relax the twisted smile on his face.

The question bounces off the walls. No one wants it. No one wants to reveal the pain that is at the heart of the riddle, which is which?, because we are all worried about the same thing, our mother, our poor mother, sinking with the weight of her years on the straight-backed chair that is hurting her bones, and all of us here, we know who is who. Even the Caboose knows it. He keeps smiling to let us know that he knows. His question is a personal victory after years of being left out. Our mother is the only one who can be hurt by it.

Our mother is the one who speaks, in a thin, faltering voice. The room holds its breath.

'Angèle died in the mine. The person you're looking at is Carmelle. Tommy.'

The truth. Finally, the truth. Spoken, revealed, freed by the one person who was supposed to be protected from it, but who is giving it back to us. Oh, Angèle! It took so long for your right to live among us to be restored.

Our father takes our mother's hand. He finds it in the folds of her dress and brings it to him, to his thigh, a slow, protective gesture. It's the first time I have seen them united, looking like a couple.

She is no longer an old woman, half lethargic, sunk in a chair. She has presence, strength – a little wobbly on her fragile ramparts, but concentrating with all her might, determined not to let this moment of lucidity pass. Because she has more, we can feel it. She won't leave us with the tenuous truth that she has just given us. She has something else to tell us. Her eyes, wide with effort, look around at her children, one by one, with her deep well of tenderness, like she used to do, and they stop at me.

'Angèle died in the mine. You know that better than any of us, Carmelle. Tell us what you saw.'

How could I have been so stupid as to believe that I had escaped our mother's eyes? She knows us better than we know ourselves. She knit us with the fibres of her soul and knows the stitch of our hearts like the back of her hand. She knew where I went to hide during your long absences, Angèle. She knew where my soul was when she came to the bedroom and saw me, eyes wide open in the night, my body vacant, and your smile full of wonder on my lips, from the happiness of seeing you living at the McDougalls' or at the convent. So she was there, that day, close to me, and she witnessed me having that horrible vision.

The Old Maid was there too. How could I forget? She is a black stain on my memory.

She is going out of her mind. She knows what our mother is asking me to do, and she wants to stop the time machine that will take us back to that horrible Sunday in July. I see her begging me with panicked eyes, dilated in fear of the worst, as if the worst hadn't already happened. No, I won't do anything to stop what must be. All these years of living with the image of Angèle dying under an avalanche of rocks, all these years of dying under the crushing weight of silence, and you want what? For me to say nothing, to bend to your will, to invent a pretty lie to quiet everyone's mind? No, you don't reign over our consciences anymore. It's time for the truth. You can't wave the spectre of our mother writhing in pain and the family torn apart. There is nothing left at the end of your stick other than the shame of having let our sister die.

I have ten pairs of eyes, twenty pairs of eyes – I can't count anymore – staring at me. They have gathered into a compact crowd and are waiting for me to speak.

I don't know where to start. So many years have passed. The silence has been so thick.

Tootsie creeps up to our mother and loosens the sad chignon that stretches the skin of her face and hardens her features, freeing her hair into two white bundles that spread over her shoulders. Any more and it would have been as though she was going to get up from her chair, the gentle flutter of the nightgown rippling in the half-light of the bedroom, and come toward me, to bend over my dreams, and my soul would at last find some respite. And I address the words that I have held back for so many years to that gentle apparition in the night.

'I saw her die, Mama. I saw it like I'm seeing you now. It wasn't a vision. I wasn't hallucinating. I was really transported to the mine, and I saw her, I felt her. I was there, beside her, inside her. I died with her.'

And I told the story. The shock wave of the first explosion, the house emptying, everyone running to the mine, and I'm there, upstairs, in the green bedroom, pressed against the wall, paralyzed in horror.

'Angèle felt the shockwave travelling through the rock. Even before the roaring started and everything came crashing down on her, she felt the force of the explosion. And she couldn't stop screaming. I screamed too when I heard her. I screamed my head off.

'She was in the mine stope, near the central pillar, and she saw the roof of the mine open up above her. Very clearly, in almost pitch black, like a film in slow motion, she saw the rock split from one end to another, huge chunks of rock breaking off and starting to fall. In a split second, she saw the rough patches and sharp edges of each rock that was going to fall on her, and, at the end of a long tunnel, she saw the eye of death awaiting her.

'I heard her bones break. I could smell her blood. I saw her heart, her lungs, her brains. But she wasn't there anymore. She died before the first rock hit her.'

I saw her escape down the long tunnel where her soul took refuge, and I knew, I felt it with all my pain, that the tunnel was off limits to me. I screamed at her to come back to me, I screamed to break down the doors of death, to force death to give Angèle back, to take me to her.

'She didn't suffer? Are you sure?'

It is the tiniest consolation our mother is clinging to. She pulls herself toward the edge of her chair and waits for my answer to pluck her from the swirling waters of doubt.

'I swear to you, Mama, Angèle didn't suffer. She didn't feel a thing. She died of fright. She died before the first rock hit her.'

I realize that I just called her Mama, a word that crept into our internal dialogues but never passed our lips. It was a word too laden with a sense of ownership to be uttered in a house like ours.

No one spots the gaffe. They are in shock, caught in a tangle of emotions, overwhelmed by a stream of images that come back to them in ways they couldn't have expected.

I am facing them, alone like always. From the teeming crowd of my brothers and sisters, pressed up against one other, not one of them holds out their hand to me. I am alone, and I won't back down, I won't be silenced. I'm being asked to speak, so I'll tell the whole story, starting with the Old Maid's grand scheme, the conspiracy she set in motion and that crushed us under the weight of a silence from which no one escaped unharmed – not even Geronimo, the very person we all wanted to shield from the hicks' condemnation and from his own sense of justice. Look at him: doesn't he look proud, our war hero? He is being eaten up by his memories. They're burning him to his core. Look around you. Do you see what you've done? We all look like zombies. We're all burning on the same fire. What was the point of forcing the silence on us?

'The Old Maid was there, in front of me, in the green bedroom. I couldn't see her. I was absorbed in the vision of Angèle under the dome of the mine stope, but I could hear her over the roar of the rocks. I heard her voice asking me, 'What is it? What's happening?' and I heard my own voice saying to her, 'Angèle ... Angèle is in the mine. In the mine stope. Beside the central pillar ... Noooooooo!' The images swooped down on me. Up against the bedroom wall, I felt every rock that crashed down on Angèle in my flesh, and, with each one, I cried, 'Run, Angèle!' but where could she have gone, since she was already dead and there was nowhere to go? And when I felt her let herself be swept into a long tunnel with blinding light, I wanted to run after her. I wanted to rip myself from the wall that was holding me prisoner, and that's when I saw the Old Maid, who was holding me with both hands and shaking me like a madwoman. She was screaming, 'Will you shut up? Will you just shut up!'

'You were coming unhinged. You should have seen yourself. You were hysterical. I couldn't stand to see you that way.'

She is wrestling with herself. She is clinging desperately to her truth. She knows what's coming. The woman is stubborn as a mule. She won't give it up that easily. She believes that she acted for the good of the family. Well, look at it now, the Cardinal family, take a good, hard look and tell me if you see anything but our own damnation.

'You forced me to put on Angèle's dress, her Sunday dress. The flowered dress, the dress that was supposed to camouflage her death. Don't try to tell me you've forgotten.

'You knew full well what you were doing and why. You kept explaining it over and over while you packed my bags, Angèle's bags. You didn't give me a second to think. You went back and forth, to the laundry room, to the bedrooms, and you just kept talking. You were trying to bury me with words while you collected her clothes, her books, everything that belonged to Angèle and that had to disappear with her, her dresses, her tunics, her white school blouses, and the McDougall woman's hat, do you remember? The hat with the feather that you got from the back of the closet, behind a pile of old catalogues? You stuffed the hat and all the rest in brown paper bags that were supposed to be Angèle's luggage, providing the proof that she was gone, "of her own choosing and never coming back." Do you remember?

'I haven't forgotten a word of what you said.

'Save the family. We have to save the family. The hicks will come, the police, the shame, prison, the pain, mother won't survive, none of us will survive. We have to be strong, stronger than the scum that wants to point the finger at us, stronger than all of it. We have to stop the others from crushing us like bugs. That's what you said.'

I couldn't have resisted her. I couldn't have torn myself away from what she was saying. She came and went, thrashing about with the fury of an animal caught in a trap. She went through every room gathering whatever might have belonged to Angèle to put a bag together for me before, on the mountain, they recovered from the surprise of the force of the blast and they all came back here, the hatred of the hicks in their wake, and before they had time to think. 'We have to face it. We have to be ready to face it.' Her voice wouldn't give me a second's rest.

It felt like an eternity in that green bedroom. I followed the trace of Angèle. I wanted to throw myself into the light that was sucking up her soul and never come back to life.

There was no point in explaining what happened next; I can see it in every pair of eyes on me. A light dress with yellow flowers stirs in the back of an old car. It rustles, it flutters, the air is pulsing with heat. A thin weak smile is formed, and they watch her disappear into the distance in a cloud of dust. Geronimo watches her up to the covered bridge. He knows he will have to meet my eyes again. Émilien bows his head. It's too much for him.

'I came back through the woods like you said to. In pants and a shirt.'

The Old Maid is destroyed. All her machinations, orchestrations, constructions, the most important work of her life, everything she did to save the family, it has all crumbled. There is no secret left, no guard on the ramparts. The Old Maid collapses into a small pile of twisted emotion.

Did she really think that all by herself, for all those years, she could hold back Angèle's soul, which was screaming to be acknowledged? It oozed out of the walls of the house. You could feel it, heavy and fraught, feeding on silence and invading our nights. Our mother gave up her nightly rounds. No one came to lean over our dark dreams. Angèle, so incredibly light while she inhabited her body, crushed us under the harsh weight of a soul full of sorrow.

I didn't last a year in the house. It was only after I left that I found the spirit's path that brought me back to my Angèle.

I swore that never again would I be forced to parade around looking like Angèle. That display in Émilien's car, while my soul was still deep in the mine, looking for Angèle, as the horror was at its peak, me in her pretty flowered dress, sitting in the back seat, alive, in good health and smiling her smile, and her, crushed to a pulp under tons of rock, that horrible charade that I had to keep up until the covered bridge … Oh Angèle! Can you ever forgive me?

In the little woods on the way home, I swore that no one would force me to smile Angèle's smile again.

The Old Maid sensed it when our eyes met in the hotel lobby. She saw that nothing could force me to make a miracle again. Only in Kangirsujuaq, in the silence of my long solitary walks, does Angèle's smile return deep in my soul.

Now that everything has been said and her spirit can rest in peace with each of us, I want to get back to my long walks by the bay, get back to Noah, his smooth, round arms around my shoulders, his warm hands, our silent conversations. I want this ceremony to be over. I want them to give our father the medal and let me live out my quiet days with the man who is waiting for me.

'You haven't told us everything …' Tintin begins, as if reading my mind.

He is in a corner, at the other end of the room, beside an enormous, monstrous philodendron that is half-hiding him. You can barely see his long silhouette and the thick tousled hair that has always been his trademark. But here in the room, we know who has just spoken. We recognize his soft, sad voice.

The compact crowd around our parents had broken up. As I emerge from my story, I see their eyes, their gestures, heavy and vague. Slowly, very slowly, they break apart and go lean against the walls.

The only ones left in the centre of the room are two old people holding each other's gnarled hand.

'You haven't told us everything,' Tintin says again, his voice more confident.

From the other end of the room, Geronimo comes to his rescue.

'He's right. You haven't told us everything. There's one question left.'

He moves toward me in an almost menacing way, because of all the trepidation inside him.

'What was Angèle doing at the mine that day?'

The question comes from I don't know whom behind him.

Like an endless echo, I hear the question hit the thin wall of their thoughts, the deafening roar that scrapes the depths of our consciousness, and from one to the other, the swell of a single voice that tells me that not one of them knows what Angèle was doing at the mine that day. How on earth is that possible? How could no one have figured it out?

While I try to come to terms with the fact that I will have to spell it out, tell them what Angèle was, our father's reedy voice cuts through the silence the room and asks the silhouette that has not left the protective shadow of the philodendron:

'And what about you, Justin, why don't you tell us what you were doing at the mine that day.'

Tintin leaves his leafy cover and starts a twisted, arduous, confused story of sticks of dynamite and feelings that don't want to be named.

'I can't remember who I was before that day. A normal kid, I suppose, happy and carefree, It was afterward that the sleepless nights and dark days started. I didn't know how to go on living. I learned again. For the others, not for me. I don't live for me anymore. I wasn't thinking of anything when I went into the mine shaft. Not even the danger. I was hoping for a good blast, that's all.'

Geronimo comes to his aid when he gets stuck, when he falters on a detail. He explains in turn, blames himself. Tintin gets annoyed and won't let him claim all the guilt. I'm barely listening. Their story doesn't matter anymore. Who laid the fatal charge? From what direction did the blast that killed her come? From the mine shaft? The lateral pillar? What does it matter since no one understands what Angèle was doing, why she had gone to the mine, her true motivation?

Once they have finished flogging themselves, it will be up to me to explain what happened. Would they finally understand? They would have to. I can't let Angèle's death be summed up by a few sticks of dynamite stuck in the rock. They would have to accept worse than Angèle's death. They would have to look at themselves, at all of us, gathered in the living room, around our hideous three-seater sofa ... Oh, Angèle! Is it possible that what happened next escaped them, that their consciousness has retained nothing of it?

I'll tell them. I will tell the story. I'll leave nothing out. That last family meeting, supposedly for Pester's birthday, but that we all knew was a war council. The last-chance meeting, because New Northern Consolidated was at our doorstep. It would swoop down on our mine and discover the tunnel that we had dug if we didn't find a way to stop it from happening. That pseudo–family celebration was the setting for our own private tragedy that led to Angèle's sacrifice.

I will spare them nothing. They will hear it all. Minute by minute, second by second, I will describe that day before Angèle's death, and then they will know that we are all, *all*, to blame for it and that there is no point in shouting the odds about the number of sticks of dynamite that this one or that one stuck in the rock.

How has their consciousness managed to escape? By what twisted road did it slither off so that nothing remains of what happened that day?

We were in the living room – well, at least everyone who really counted in the family was there. Geronimo, Big Yellow and Fakir, our most ardent speechifiers, settled in to the discomfort of the sofa, a place of choice in spite of the springs that poked through between the divots and the bumps. Beside them, perched crookedly on the arm of the sofa, was Tintin, listening carefully to everything that was being said. And on the other arm of the sofa was Matma. Who else was there? The Old Maid, of course, leaning against the kitchen door-frame, her usual spot. Mustang and Yahoo, straddling chairs in the middle of the room. Behind them, Tut and Magnum, perched on what originally must have been a kitchen counter, now used to store a colossal mess. And in the corner, near the TV, Émilien, silent and gloomy, hiding behind a cloud of ciga-rette smoke.

In fact, the whole day, the evening and part of the night, there were constant comings and goings, agitation that spread from the living room to the kitchen, from the kitchen to upstairs. Not a room in the house was spared the unrest of this major gathering which, after Pester's traditional blasting at the sand quarry, led us into endless discussions about remaking the world in our image. As the conversation ebbed, this time, a much more immediate concern came up: how to prevent New North-ern Consolidated from sticking its nose in our tunnel.

Only the youngest were left out of the discussion. They were outside most of the time, rapt in fascination over all the cars parked in front of the house, five or six wheezing, coughing beaters that the Big Kids had driven back from the big city. Outside, Nefertiti, Wapiti, Tootsie and the Caboose were singing themselves hoarse as they drove down imaginary roads: the roar of the engine, the screech of the tires, the clank of the metal. Even when they honked the horns in unison, no one inside said a word about the commotion.

Between the fervour of our discussions and the racket made by the Weewuns circulated those without status in the family, so to speak: too young for the Big Kids, too old for the Weewuns, they couldn't sit still. El Toro, whom we should have called Snoopy on account of his curiosity, was everywhere all at once.

Our father put in an appearance in the living room at the end of the evening. Angèle's fate had already been sealed. It happened just after supper. Did the Old Man, buried in his basement, and our mother, nearby, in the kitchen, understand what was happening? I was there, in the eye of the storm, and I didn't grasp the extent of it until it was too late. Angèle had made up her mind.

We were there, every one of us who was looking in the lull of the conversation to ward off the calamity that would come crashing down on our family. The threat emerged regularly, silent and hostile, in the heated debates. The crushing feeling of powerlessness was overwhelming, because the clock was ticking, and we hadn't found a way to protect our tunnel from the inquisitive eye of New Northern Consolidated.

This is the point in the story where Angèle makes up her mind. Lord up above or down below, give my words force because now I have to approach shores filled with quicksand and misunderstandings. How can I make them understand?

As usual, Angèle and I were side by side, sitting on the floor against the wall facing the sofa. Neither of us had said a word during the discussion. We wouldn't have dared. Words were reserved first for the occupants of the sofa, who debated all topics with equal authority. The others jumped in when they felt the floor was open, and then there was a heated clash of arguments that reminded us of a time not so long ago when we were the kings of Norco and nothing could touch us. And just like in the good old days, someone would get up to visit the bathroom or just to stretch their legs, with a resounding *Smyplace*, accompanied by a bit of buffoonery or a triumphant fart.

How could I make them understand that Angèle didn't mean to reject the family or any of its codes, that she didn't mean to offend or defy anyone when she got up and rather than the *Smyplace* we would normally expect, she said, clearly and distinctly, each word tolling the bell for her, 'That's my place.'

I don't know what she was thinking. I don't even know if she *was* thinking when she did such a stupid, senseless thing.

It was an unspeakable insult. Coming from anyone but her, it would have just been a joke, a witticism without consequences, but the thin thread Angèle had been dangling from for so many years couldn't hold up to such acrobatics. Did she want to test the thread's strength? Did she want to find out to just how much she belonged to this family?

The sentence was stiff, merciless and without appeal. No hearts went out to her. Not even mine. I was frozen, my eyes cast down at the floor. My final betrayal.

A deafening silence swept across the living room, one end to the other. A stinging absence of heart. Angèle was standing in the middle of us, tortured, waiting for a sharp, biting word, a nasty remark of some sort to fly from some direction and deliver her from what seemed like an eternity. Nothing came. The silence was her punishment, her sentence.

I was a breath away from her. I could have touched her just by moving my hand, only slightly, barely a twitch, not even a gesture. Nobody would have seen it, and she would have had someone to hang on to, someone who could have grabbed her as life was slipping from under her feet. But I did nothing. I too was under the spell of the affront, and the sentence. I was hangman and victim. I was mired in mixed feelings. I was a coward yet again. Angèle, can you ever forgive me?

The silence spread like a storm through the house. The Weewuns stopped their racket. No one was running on the stairs anymore. There wasn't a sound anywhere. Time stood still. Angèle looked around at each of us, looking for a crack in the wall of condemnation and, not finding it, she left the living room with a decided step. She had made up her mind.

How could we have been so blind?

With her certain step, she went to load up on dynamite to blow up the central pillar of the mine. She was so gentle and swanlike, but she was going to sneak into the great cave of the mine and with her dainty hands, tie a string of dynamite around the pillar and wait for the explosion to free her.

She knew full well what she was doing. Since her visit to the mine with Geronimo, she understood the importance of the central pillar, but she thought she was alone in this tragic endeavour. And when Geronimo and Tintin each arrived with the heedlessness of conquerors, they didn't realize that Angèle was one step ahead of them. It was a horrible twist of fate.

She didn't commit suicide. She sacrificed herself. She set herself on fire at the family altar. To save us all and to make amends for an offence she had not committed. To seal her belonging to the Cardinal clan forever. Angèle, can you ever forgive us?

Jocelyne **Saucier** was born in New Brunswick and lives in Abitibi, Québec. Two of her previous novels, *La vie comme une image* (*House of Sighs*) and *Jeanne sur les routes* (*Jeanne's Road*) were finalists for the Governor General's Award. *Il pleuvait des oiseaux* (*And the Birds Rained Down*) garnered her the Prix des Cinq continents de la Francophonie, making her the first Canadian to win the award. The book was a CBC Canada Reads Selection in 2015.

Rhonda Mullins is a writer and translator living in Montréal. *And the Birds Rained Down*, her translation of Jocelyne Saucier's *Il pleuvait des oiseaux*, was a CBC Canada Reads Selection. It was also shortlisted for the Governor General's Literary Award, as were her translations of Élise Turcotte's *Guyana* and Hervé Fischer's *The Decline of the Hollywood Empire*.

Typeset in Albertan.

Albertan was designed by the late Jim Rimmer of New Westminster, B.C., in 1982. He drew and cut the type in metal at the 16pt size in roman only; it was intended for use only at his Pie Tree Press. He drew the italic in 1985, designing it with a narrow fit and a very slight incline, and created a digital version. The family was completed in 2005, when Rimmer redrew the bold weight and called it Albertan Black. The letterforms of this type family have an old-style character, with Rimmer's own calligraphic hand in evidence, especially in the italic.

Printed at the old Coach House on bpNichol Lane in Toronto, Ontario, on Zephyr Antique Laid paper, which was manufactured, acid-free, in Saint-Jérôme, Quebec, from second-growth forests. This book was printed with vegetable-based ink on a 1965 Heidelberg KORD offset litho press. Its pages were folded on a Baumfolder, gathered by hand, bound on a Sulby Auto-Minabinda and trimmed on a Polar single-knife cutter.

Edited and designed by Alana Wilcox
Cover design by Ingrid Paulson
Photo of Jocelyne Saucier by Cyclopes
Photo of Rhonda Mullins by Owen Egan

Coach House Books
80 bpNichol Lane
Toronto ON M5S 3J4
Canada

416 979 2217
800 367 6360

mail@chbooks.com
www.chbooks.com